WITHDRAWN

MANNEQUIN

BOOKS
by
FANNIE HURST

MANNEQUIN

APPASSIONATA

EVERY SOUL HATH ITS SONG

GASLIGHT SONATAS

HUMORESQUE

LUMMOX

STAR DUST

THE VERTICAL CITY

MANNEQUIN

by

Fannie Hurst

(Mrs. Jacques S. Danielson)
1889-

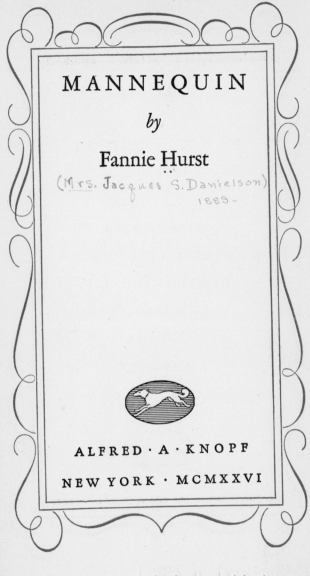

ALFRED · A · KNOPF

NEW YORK · MCMXXVI

BOOK I

BOOK I

MANNEQUIN

I

THERE was an orchid that grew in the window-box of Selene Herrick. Tender thing, it had been transplanted in among the hardinesses of geranium and of bachelor-button and phlox without a thought that it could survive more than its one bloom. And there it was, persistently lifting its head toward the city light.

A head the colour of smeared sunset.

Selene tended that flower with finger-tips as delicate as the flesh of the petals themselves. She was like that. With a capacity for infinite pains for coaxing beauty.

The first year that John Lester Herrick was married to her he had occasion to know that fact. But, strangely enough, a little bitterly.

Sometimes it seemed to John Lester, who loved her, that a swift river-current, made up of things and things and things, was carrying her downstream from him. A current made up of the things that Selene loved. Italian trip-tychs. Orchids with mauve flesh. Spanish velvets that looked as if they were woven out

[3]

of the red of burning altar-lamps. Lingerie. Baby-dresses made by the tender hands of nuns. Brocatelles. Credenzas with solemn basilica doors carved with figures of the Apostles, as they loved to do them in the seventeenth century. Fine linen. Yellow Wedgwood. Tapestries with wrong sides to be proud of. Florentine book-ends. Brittany ware. Tiffany glass. Faïence goblets. A mezzotint portrait of a lady. View of the exterior of Windsor Castle. A pair of marquetry commodes that had lost their legs but not their fine design.

It was a dream, or rather a nightmare, that sometimes persisted through into the reality of John Lester's workaday.

Things. Things. Things. Cloisonné. Marquetry. Flutings of mahogany and linen fold of walnut. Selene, who loved things, floating away from him on a stream of them.

She would have been the first to laugh and smooth away this phantasmagoria from the tired brow of her husband.

If Selene loved things, part of that love was her urge to enhance the background of this serious-minded, entirely artless mate of hers, whom she believed, with an artlessness that far transcended his indifference to the material world of credenzas and ball-bearing perambulators, to be destined for high place.

[4]

MANNEQUIN

High place.

There was never an evening, beholding John Lester with his rough brown head down over his law-books, that the reality of him would not fade out, and Selene, bent on the other side of the table over handiwork too fine for even her strong young eyes, would visualize him, this great cub-like young husband of hers, austere in some rôle of high estate.

Corporation lawyer. Mayor. Senator.

Sometimes, when Selene etched her picture of John Lester's future in words, they laughed over it. But never quite sincerely.

It was a dream that was as real to one as to the other. The rôle of district attorney. Corporation lawyer; even — well, even the imagination of Selene had its faltering-point.

*

That was why from the very start, notwithstanding John Lester's rather stodgy inability to realize it, their little apartment in a building of one hundred and nine identically like it, was yet not like them. With a cleverness due to Selene, not like them.

The one hundred and nine three-piece living-room-suites, piano floor-lamps, cabinet victrolas. Flemish oak dining-rooms, twin beds, balcony-front dressers with glass tops that repeated themselves in vertical layers up and down the steep apartment-lined streets of the Upper West Side.

The apartments of thousands of the standardized young families of the American commonwealth. Backbone-of-the-nation families. Statistic-builders. Willing products of the biscuit-tin system of standardization. Standardization of morals, furniture, derby hats, salad-dressing, velour upholstery, churches, colleges, amusements, silk stockings, morning cereal, and morning headlines.

One after another of the homes of the commonwealth. Family victrolas in mahogany cabinets. Family measles. Family servant problems. Family ambitions. Family skeletons. Family budgets. Family toothbrush-holders marked 1, 2, 3. Family made-in-Grand-Rapids dining-room tables with a fern dish for centre and a dome of many-coloured glass overhead.

Row after row, layer after layer of the backbone of the nation.

And there, jammed in the layers, Selene's home. A little outstanding. A little different.

Old John Lester — the difference, however, was of no great moment to him. A Spanish credenza for his shirts and collars was all right if it mattered one way or another to Selene,

but a good old-fashioned chiffonier would have
been a darned sight more comfortable.

Old John Lester. There you have it. When
John was twenty-six and in the first twenty-
two months of his married life, it came
natural to call him that. *Old John Lester.* It
was not that he did not have youth. Indeed
he had it. Of a great sprawling, cubbish kind.
It must have been because of his six-feet-one
and the bulk of shoulders that went with it,
and the dark good conscientious-looking eyes
of him. Good old St. Bernard eyes. There you
were again. Old John Lester. One meant,
rather, fine, sincere, honest, and impeccable
John Lester. And talented John Lester.

He was each and every one of these, and no
one knew it better than Selene, with her clear
grey eyes fixed on mounting against proper
background this man of hers who was so irref-
utably destined for high place.

There was a game that used to take place
over the top of the head of the orchid in its
box, through the upper pane of one of the
bow-windows of their dining-room, so that the
tender cup of the orchid and the equally tender
cup of Selene's chin almost touched.

Across the roofs and clotheslines that inter-
vened between Riverside Drive, Selene, by a
judicious tiptoeing and craning of neck, could

catch a gleam of the Hudson River and the parade of the Palisades beyond.

"Close one eye, John, and squint the other. Now, look! Can't you just imagine it's the Riviera, or one of those estates up around Tarrytown that we pass on the train coming down from Peekskill? No, no, darling stupid, you! Don't close both eyes. There! See, this is a screen of orchids growing on our terrace, and that pent-house over on that roof is a pergola. . . ."

Usually John kissed her or tweaked the lobe of her ear to these flights of her fancy, or just as frequently snapped open his evening paper.

Life was so full of the concrete things of the moment. Eager, crowding, close, actual things such as Juvenile Court Reform bill, or the forthcoming primaries, or the decision handed down on the Meighan case by the Court of Appellate Division.

Difficult tricky case, that! How John would have liked to handle it. Lee Meighan was guilty!

Sometimes, in pantomime, after Selene was in bed, John Lester rehearsed what his summing-up before the jury would have been in the Meighan case. . . .

These fantasies of Selene's lay outside the safe and snug harbour of the practical realities of John's affairs. The realities of indirect primaries, Federal Reserve Banks systems, the drawing up of wills, a paper on mass criminology which he was preparing for a law journal.

Life was so full of the concrete demands of the immediate!

No one knew better than Selene, however, how obscuring, to even such flights of fancy as she allowed herself, were the demands of the concrete and the immediate.

The demands of the immediate. Selene knew them, all right. Here were a few of them:

There were four of Joan's little made-by-Selene's-hand dresses, lying now in just the necessary and mixed-by-Selene's-hand suds to enhance their whiteness. They should be rinsed and hung to dry immediately. Except that John Lester's dinner chops were broiling, and, because he liked them with the fat on, they sizzled too rapidly to be left for more than just the time for the peep above the indescribably tender flesh of the orchid, to where the Hudson River showed itself for that instant between the chimney-pots.

Indeed, Selene knew the demands of the immediate! She could not have managed to eke out of the not-so-rising income of a rising young lawyer the impeccable, fastidious little apartment, had she not known them.

MANNEQUIN

Part of knowing them was such strange wisdoms as these:

By mixing a pound of seventy-five-cent coffee with a pound of thirty-nine-cent grade, one could achieve, almost, the flavour of a famous eighty-cent brand.

The basement of a certain Fourteenth Street department store yielded an excellent domestic cotton damask that, by lamplight, at least, gave off something of the rich low lustre of Italian brocatelle.

Just ordinary talcum powder could do wonders toward keeping spotless the adorable little square-toed white boots of an eighteen-months-old little girl.

If one had the patience and the leisure, and a sufficiently driving distaste for machine-made domestic furniture (Selene had!), auction rooms, luck along, could yield up fantastically low-priced bits that bore the mysterious patina of years and foreign lands.

The way to keep a baby girl's little dimity dresses as sheer-looking as the fine linen ones of the children one saw wheeled out by their nurses on the eastern side of the Mall, is to drop just enough of a patented starch into the water to give the fabric sheen without stiffness.

Astrakhan, if one can only find the short-nap,

silky grade, makes up almost as handsomely for a perambulator cover as Persian lamb.

A woman with few evening dresses and a faint luminous glow to her neck and arms will do well to see that those few are black.

An extraordinary champagne punch can be made out of two-thirds tea.

If trousers are hung upside-down, they fall into crease almost as if newly pressed.

Two aspirin tablets in the water of a vase of flowers will keep cut flowers fresh for a week.

These were only some of the little wisdoms that were so strangely Selene's own. They were as saliently and characteristically her own as the grey-green of her eyes and the jade white of her skin. A skin that, one felt when groping around to determine why Selene's beauty somehow fell just short, should have contrasted with hair as black as John Lester's, rather than with the tawny ash of Selene's own.

In little Joan this contrast was achieved. In Selene's baby girl, straight black wing-like hair lay against a pallor of skin that had somewhere in its pigmentation a cunning admixture of green.

A little black-pearl quality that made Joan exotic at two.

Evenings, while John Lester pored over the

law volumes and his books of psychology, pathology, and sociology that were closely related to his growing interest in the study of crime, Selene, in an authentic little Spanish chair purchased at auction, bent her eyes over the exacting needlework of little-girl dresses.

But the reward for the eye-strain and the back-ache lay in wheeling Joan in her ball-bearing perambulator out in these daintinesses of her own handiwork and beholding passer-by after passer-by turn in delighted admiration.

What a beautiful baby!

Oh, you darling lovely child! Little girl, of course, isn't she?

See that exquisite baby! What curious and lovely colouring.

Oh, did you see that beautiful baby we just passed?

The gratification to Selene, wheeling her, was one of possession and achievement.

Gratifications which also shone back at her from her pride in the little apartment.

One wondered, beholding Selene in the particular layer of the one she called home, there in that great hive of one hundred and ten, just why hers was not identical with the twelve stories of Axminster rugs, Nottingham curtains, and spick-and-span new bright-red-ma-

hogany-with-plate-glass-top dining-room tables that must have adorned at least ten of the
eleven dining-rooms above and below hers.

Selene's dining-room table was an Italian
walnut gate-leg. Even with a sag in the wood,
it was a particularly good one. Indeed, as
things go in the minds of the antique-mongers,
that sag in the wood made it a table to be
coveted. Selene had dug it out of a second-
hand shop in Fourth Avenue; and the very
next week a dealer, delivering her a pair of iron
dogs for her gas grate, had offered her one-third
again what she paid for it.

One wondered how she knew, there in the
layers of the furniture-factory dining-room
"sets." The Stoke-on-Trent pottery on her
side-board, completely out of period, blended
so perfectly. Her imitation Sheffield was right.
Selene knew in the surest, subtlest way. With
her instinct. Just as she had known, in the
up-the-river town of Peekskill, to refer to her
father, who laid most of his bricks by hand,
as a contractor rather than a builder, and to
eliminate the family napkin-rings in an era
when Battenberg needlework was the reigning
indoor pastime.

With her instinct Selene knew. Her instinct
to be fastidious.

There was a Sheraton buffet in her little

dining-room — an authentic piece of exceptionally fine hand turning, picked up in battered condition at a ridiculously low price in a second-hand shop and restored, by the combined efforts of herself and a neighbourhood cabinet-maker, to its original lustre.

A bit of tapestry hung over that buffet, of weave almost as cunning as Flemish, with a Merovingian king and his consorts riding across a plain of fine perspectives.

And over that tapestry hung a tale.

The tale of one of the few angry scenes of the twenty-two months of her married life with John Herrick. The kind of scene that was to lie heavily at Selene's heart for days after her husband had not only forgiven, but forgotten.

*

It was not, after all, so very much of a scene. More than likely, many such took place nightly in the twelve layers of the one hundred and ten apartments of the Upper West Side building known as Priscilla Court.

Presently John Lester, who loved to kiss the light tan hair of Selene because to his lips it felt warm and sweet as hay, was to kiss away the scene between them. But, as John Lester told her while his anger was upon him and the furrow out between his eyes, that came there only when the household budget was up for discussion, the cost of that bit of tapestry was two-thirds of his month's earnings. Sweat and sinew that John Lester needed for the homelinesses of butter-and-egg bills and shoes for little Joan and rent and gas and ice had soaked into the rag of thing called tapestry that had precipitated the scene between them.

The inanimate power of a bit of thing to precipitate bitterness into one instant of his relations with this woman who was his, was what riled John Lester as much as anything. That one piece of tapestry-smear across a wall had not only cost him two-thirds of his entire month's earnings, but more, shamefully more, in nausea of spirit and mind.

Selene's love of things. Sometimes after she had gone to bed, pretty well exhausted what with her household puttering all day and an evening over the infinitesimal needlework, John Lester, book fallen forward on his knees and resting his tired eyes by pressing his fingers against the give of his eyeballs as his mind peregrinated through the maze of struggle-for-existence problems, could ponder and ponder on this quality in the woman he loved.

Love of things. The smothering threat of them, as of shields and of bracelets falling in a shower that would presently smother them.

Inanimate things that could never mean more than a certain gratification of the bazaar instinct in woman. Love of things.

John Lester, even then deep in the work which later was to distinguish him, used sometimes to look upon this mate of his as if seeing her for the first time.

Love of things. It made him, in his pity for her, because of the vast vistas that were closed to her — the vistas of his pilgrimages into the dark, the remote, the attic places of the human mind — a little more lenient, a little more tolerant; and, incongruously enough, of course, after each of these crashes over the household budget, a little more in love.

Pity for Selene. She would have smiled at that.

*

Because, if ever a man needed tending and managing, John Lester did. That had been obvious to her the first day she clapped eyes on him, at a strawberry fête at Peekskill, where he practised law with a native Peekskill boy, their first year out of college. And management by someone clever enough to keep him a little sorry for her. Selene Herrick's eyes were not that clear grey for nothing. They were the eyes of a head that can think coolly.

And yet it required no particularly clear

thinking or subtle appraisement to learn to
reckon with John Lester in terms of achievement. He was so obviously the timber of success. It was writ in those steady, dogged, con-
scientious eyes of his. In the wide, ready white
smile of the congenital good mixer. Fanatical
love of his job. Preparation for it. Genius for
it. John Lester, aided and abetted, would go
far. Subtly aided and abetted, so that John
Lester, thinking of his wife, would think of
her with the mist of that certain wistful pity
for her across his eyes. A wistful adoring kind
of sympathy for weaknesses that after all, in
Selene, were adorable.

Yes, John Lester, properly and subtly aided
and abetted, would go far.

There was the Garfinkle case.

In her heart, it gave Selene a glow that John
Lester, a struggling lawyer with just one
slightly conspicuous case to his credit, and that
one which had fallen to him by accident of
mistaken names, should dare to refuse the
Garfinkle case.

It made her glow, to be married to a man
with the superb kind of intellectual courage
and integrity, even insolence, to be able to do
that.

At a time, too, when the first rungs of the
ladder toward John's achievement had proved

so consistently unattainable, like one of those comedy treadmills that keep throwing the donkey off.

She paid for the glow, though, that came with his courage in forfeiting the Garfinkle case, with the forfeiting of her most secret and immediate ambition.

The ambition of being able to afford a nursemaid! But just the same, if you were Selene Herrick with the cool grey eyes of cool thinking, you were none the less proud. Proud of John Lester's renunciation.

John Lester believed young Garfinkle guilty of the unsavoury charge against him. And with the great Garfinkle fortune prepared to go the limit for exoneration, John Lester, in his great big slow, rather dogged manner, dared to refuse a case which would have meant important public recognition, whichever way the wind of decision had blown.

And Selene stood by her husband's decision. A little grandly, she thought. After all, inevitably in the career of a man whose affairs would have ultimately to do with big things and big decisions and big political and legal affairs, John Herrick would sooner or later have to learn his bitter lesson of compromise.

"No!" thundered John.

"I hope you're right, dear."

Strange quality in Selene, with her little earthy turn of head, that she should want to stave off for John the possibility of the day of his first reconciliation to compromise.

She counterbalanced it, though, in a sly little obvious fashion that caused even John Lester, in his slow way, to smile. Funny, cunning combination of child and wiseacre, this Selene of his.

Long after the decision to renounce the Garfinkle case had been reached, it was Selene who had insisted that he seek out men like Judge Rhincoop, who even then was looking favourably upon young Herrick, and like Herbert Wing, probably the outstanding corporation lawyer of his time, who had once asked John Lester to sit at his table at a Bar Association banquet.

Selene wanted these men to know, at least, the tidbit that could have fallen into John Lester's lap, and of his refusal. Selene wanted John Lester in the foreconsciousness of men like these. It took the bitterness off the edge of the immediate renunciation.

Selene's share of the renunciation, when she stood by so grandly, was the nurse-maid.

The Garfinkle case would have meant that the Herricks could afford one. And Selene wanted a nurse-maid. It was amazing, her

capacity for wanting. With the whole of her
being Selene yearned for a nurse-maid. In uniform.

*

It was not that the actual flesh-and-blood
nurse-girl about the house would have meant
so much; although, even with Selene's fine
young vitality, endurance could sag under the
complex performance that those four little fastidious rooms and the doings of a baby daughter could make out of a day. To say nothing
of the fact that it was impossible to eke out of
the routine so much as a free afternoon for
shopping unless her mother, a large amiable
woman of creamy, fragrant-looking flesh, and
incredibly talkative, came all the way in from
Peekskill to care for little Joan in her absence.

What Selene actually wanted, though, with
a passion that had its amusing side, was not so
much the nurse-maid to help her with the
really back-hurting chores of keeping her tiny
daughter Joan the sheerest, the most delecta-
ble child in one hundred and ten apartments
of them. Chiefly, mind you, Selene wanted a
nurse-maid in uniform. The kind of uniform
that would enhance the loveliness of Joan.

She never visualized her without the uniform. A black sateen one with crisp white
organdie bows, like listening dog-ears. Selene

knew how to turn such bows, carefully, by hand. One made them with a little rolled edge. It was pleasant to watch Selene's fastidious fingers step in among such handiwork as the organdie bows.

And Selene, with a passion that had its amusing side, wanted Joan wheeled out afternoons by a smart automaton-looking nursemaid like the ones that wheeled their charges in battleship-grey perambulators out of the stone lace Renaissance homes that bordered Central Park on the extreme opposite side from the one on which the Herricks lived.

There was already the perambulator, purchased second-hand but re-enamelled a battleship grey, and into the nest of made-by-Selene's-hand pillows Joan fitted. Exquisitely.

Among countless other gratifications of body and spirit, the Garfinkle case would have meant the crowning touch of a nurse-maid.

That is why Selene thought that she stood by rather grandly.

There is a line from Emerson which Selene had once used in a high-school essay. She had never read the text from which the quotation was taken. But she recited it quite glibly upon frequent occasion. It used to amuse John Lester. Dear little fraud. Wanting to seem erudite.

At first John Lester had been impressed, and

then had fallen in love quickly enough to find the sham, after he discovered it, adorable.

The line from Emerson had to do with compensation. Selene believed in the immutability of that law.

It asserted itself one day in a fashion that delighted her. Less than three months after the incident of the Garfinkle decision, another plum of a case, not so conspicuous perhaps, but splendidly remunerative, came John Lester's way.

Secretly Selene preened herself upon her part in the achievement. It was indirectly the result of a growing friendship which she was ever so subtly fostering between John Lester and Herbert Wing.

But, be that as it may, it was on a blustery, none too propitious, but memorable November day that Selene, with the nervous excitement of thrill running high in her, set out for Panatcost's Intelligence Office in search of a nursemaid.

II

There was something about Annie Pogany that made you think at first you were seeing a little dimly. As if a mirror had been breathed on. Or as if your own eyes watered. There was that kind of haze to her eyes, which were blue but sort of smeared off, like rubbed crayon, into the whites. Her hair did that, too. Straggled off. Amber-coloured hair tucked up under a hat that was almost a comedy hat. A sailor that sat rather high, even in a day when hats rode grandly on the tops of pompadours.

One turned to look at Annie, shabby there on her bench in the park. There was that in her face, rather a poor yearning face of none too quick wits, that arrested you. In its way, paradoxically enough, it was a burning face. A face with a fever. Something startled, something hungry, something flaming in the smear of eyes and hair, and as if seen through the glass darkly, that arrested one.

It arrested the children who came from the Fifth Avenue side of the park with their uniformed nurse-maids and lunged about the Mall on roller-skates. They stood in little clumps to stare. Chiefly, perhaps, because when Annie stared back from over the top of her newspaper, which was folded the narrow width of one of its want-ad columns, her own eyes seemed to overflow at them. Not exactly of tears. But of wanting something.

Annie Pogany had the face of desperately, passionately wanting something. Children were the first to sense that. They stood and stared back. Round-eyed. Clumps of three or four of them at a time, teetering on their skates, until their nurse-maids shooed them with clapping of hands and nodding of the dog-eared bows.

Tangibly, what Annie Pogany was wanting was a job. But if you sat on a bench and jabbed a hairpin into the addresses of "Nursemaids Wanted," in the newspaper that was folded over to the narrow width of a Help Wanted–Female column, you did not accomplish much by following them up.

That is, if you were shabby and had the wistful indeterminate face of Annie Pogany.

It was the references that were the most bothersome. All the stone lace houses with their Renaissance fronts opened their rapid fire of questionings with that one first: References? Annie Pogany had one. A letter that was breaking a little at the creases from handling.

Chiefly from being handed back to her in a gesture of dismissal.

The nurse-maids she encountered in the park, the smart edge of the park where the children were the best dressed, were not very helpful. They merely stared at her, most of them, if she asked a question, or drew their children in a brood about them and passed on. Or sat in little groups of battleship-grey ball-bearing perambulators with frothings of fur and lingerie coverings.

It was like being on the edge of any other social group. Annie Pogany, who looked, in some curious inexplicable way, the rather furtive fact that she had been born on a barge of a fishwife mother and no particular father, simply did not belong to the tidy groups. Once one of the grand ones from this social stratum of domestic help did sit down on the bench beside Annie, while her charges, two sturdy boys in brown leather leggings and mink fur reefers, darted on roller-skates. She sat down for the moment and for the immediate reason that the organdie bow to her nurse's bonnet needed adjusting. Poor Annie Pogany. She lost no time edging in with a question.

How did one go about obtaining a position to nurse two such lovely charges?

One didn't just go about it. One was trained.

Oh.

References?

Well, yes. Annie Pogany had them. One, at least. The one that was thumbed from being handed back in the gesture of dismissal. —

Redfern School for Girls,
Taverin Island, N. Y.

To Whom it may Concern:

Annie Pogany has had a course in domestic science in this institution and has been honourably discharged from same.

May Hatton, *Matron.*

"You call that a reference? Why, you're out
of a reform school. You poor thing, that's like
bragging about your honourable discharge
from Sing Sing. You've been trying to prove
that you're a bad girl by showing your certifi-
cate, haven't you? Oh, say, I didn't think
they came thataway any more."

"It's a school for girls without homes that
want to learn trades."

"Yeh, maybe it is, but you forget it. Try
Panatcost's or any of the Sixth Avenue intelligence offices where your word is as good as
your reference. And believe me, it won't take
much of a word to be as good as that reference
of yours. Redfern School for Girls — and she
brags about it! And she lives, too, and bats
her eyes and knows enough to know it isn't
raining, because she hasn't got her umbrella
up."

*

The Sixth Avenue intelligence offices. There
were so many of them that sometimes they set
her eyes spinning until the street seemed yards
and yards of one after another of them, unfurl-
ing like a strip of carpet.

She stood in throngs outside them and read
off blackboards:

Wanted: 1 second butler. 4 chauffeurs for
country work. 1 cook for lunch wagon. 2 girls

for general housework, city. Man and wife for chauffeur and cook. 4 laundresses. 5 nurse-girls. 1 gardener.

Sometimes she entered and sat in a dim clot of faces back against the walls of outer offices that were the stale colour and smell of old pools.

Sometimes she just moved aimlessly from one bit of blackboard to the next.

The unrolling strip of carpet of all the intelligence offices.

It seemed no use. Time and time again being called before this prospective employer and that. Housekeepers engaging a "staff." Matrons of Institutions with the dreaded odour of lysol about them, out after help. Landladies. Women with waiting motor cars and lovely little creeping scents of perfume to them. In a way it was absurd to hope to qualify if your features were not set in your face neatly and precisely as the features of "trained help" somehow always were, and if your coat had a great threadbare stain all the way down the front, and your hat, with a single rose on a rickety stem, had been bought off a push-cart in Delancey Street and somehow had a comedy look to it.

The demand, even if you were willing to ac-

cept lower wages, much lower, was for trained
help. Young mothers in search of nurse-maids
looked at her face, as through the mist, and at
the stain of threadbare down her coat and the
shoes that had lopped from a careening way of
walking, and passed on.

And yet, day after day, somehow, Annie held
out against the little men with the grease-caked
waistcoats — the janitors of office buildings
and empty houses, who were always wanting
to engage her on the spot as charwoman and
send her to the corner to purchase pails and lye
and disinfectants.

If you wanted desperately, more than anything, and with a starveling's capacity for
wanting, to be nurse-maid to a lovely baby,
you held out stubbornly, down to the very last
penny in your petticoat pocket, against the
rôle of charwoman and the days of walking on
knees across the splintery floors of old buildings.

Once so much as let a single crack eat its way
into her hand, and then sure enough, relent-
lessly, inevitably, Annie knew it would mean
that she was ruthlessly outside the pale. The
pale of the golden babies who sometimes held
out their arms to her and crowed when she
passed them in the park.

And so, with the letter from Redfern buried

deeply inside her bodice, she held out stubbornly day after day in the outer rooms of the intelligence offices that had written on their blackboards "Wanted: Nurse-maids."

It seemed incredible that this young mother, with a scent to her that was a faint tickle to the senses, was actually engaging her. The most fastidious, almost, of all the long line of them who had eyed her that morning. In a plush coat that looked the richness of dark deep fur, even though it did not quite feel it, and the clearest, loveliest pallor that matched up with the smooth grey eyes. It was true Annie was being shaved down a little, even on the modest wage she asked, by the smooth-toned voice that matched the eyes.

As if it mattered, though, being shaved down when a young matron with a scent to her was engaging her as nurse-maid to an eighteen-months-old little girl.

She stood with her hands clasped over the stain of threadbare down her coat, trying hard not to blink her eyes in a nervous way she had under excitement.

It was a compromise to Selene Herrick to have to pass by the obviously better-trained-and-equipped applicants in the office. But, gracious, the wages they asked! They were entirely prohibitive to the lean indulgence she

and John Lester were allowing themselves in
engaging a nurse-maid.

After all, though, there was something meek
and submissive about this girl that made it
seem possible to train her. None too bright,
apparently, and certainly none too likely in
appearance. And yet, by squinting at her so
that the frowsy creature faded a little, Selene
could visualize her in the uniform, the black
sateen one with the organdie bows. If only
she loved babies and was willing to learn!
Those, after all, were the important qualifications. And apparently this rather curious
shabby creature had both.

The rest, the quick and calculating brain of
Selene could take care of.

And so, debonairly, as always, Selene went
down to her compromise.

*

That evening a great scissors went squawk-
ing across a sewing-table, so that John Lester,
crouched over a History of the Jukes Family,
laid his hands to his ears to shut out the grating noises of slightly rusty steel.

Squinting her eyes repeatedly in her effort to
recall, it seemed to Selene that the measurements of the new nurse-maid, due to arrive the
following morning, must be so-and-so and

such-and-such. And so, far into the night, long after John Lester had dragged the bolt across the front door, emptied the ice-pan, placed the empty milk-bottles on the dumb-waiter, tweaked out the front hall light, and called to her to raise the window and come to bed, Selene stitched on. At the black sateen uniform she was making from her memory of the measurements of Annie Pogany; and at the white organdie bows which, by a little trick of rolling the edges, Selene knew how to make stand upright.

*

The long days. The proud days. It did not matter that her charge lived on the wrong side of the park from the flocks of the perambulators of the smartly trained nurse-maids, or that in order to get little Joan's carriage in and out of the narrow elevator of Priscilla Court one had to manœuvre endlessly with the rear wheels. Once started on the promenade with her, that walk became a triumphal march.

There did not seem to be a woman able to pass little Joan in her lingerie nest of pillows and the white astrakhan coach-cover that looked like Persian lamb, without a pause, a gasp, and a squeal.

Literally, it was a procession strewn with

the ejaculations of the admiration of the passer-by.

It made Annie Pogany in her black sateen, with the perkiness of the little bows, walk with her head thrust forward and a briskness not usually hers, out in her careening walk. It made Selene, peering from her high window after them as far as the eye could reach, quicken of heart-beat.

There was never a time, in the elevator or on the Mall or crossing a street, that someone did not pause to inquire the parentage of Joan. Not a day but Annie came home with this and that recital of this and that incident. Some days, in the afternoons, which were free now for Selene to browse to her heart's content in and out among the shops that she loved, she deliberately crossed through the park, ostensibly for a glimpse of her Joan, but actually for the vain little purpose — the purpose she used to admit, with her cheek up against John Lester's — of hearing the nurse-maids on the benches and the mothers sitting out with their embroidery, while their children romped, point her out as the mother of Joan.

Well, there was a certain amount of pardonable pride in that.

When Joan Herrick, at two years of age, looked out at you with grey resplendent eyes of health from under a sombre black curtain of hair, and, likely as not, crowed at you and reached out two arms of that pearl-fleshed pallor of hers, your heart-strings twitched.

Annie's did. There never seemed a moment of her taking for granted the loveliness of this charge that was hers. She used to feed her eyes on it while little Joan slept. She used, sitting in her cubby-hole of a room evenings, while Selene and John Lester played with their offspring the last hour before bed, to sit waiting to be called to undress her and all the time visualizing, through closed eyes, the loveliness that she grudged to surrender to the parents for even the brief romp before bed.

It made the inexperience, the shortcomings, the clumsiness of Annie a little more endurable. Her pride in little Joan. In Selene's mind, at least, it covered a multitude of sins. It was John Lester, never horrid with help or subordinates as a rule, who could seem strangely horrid with Annie.

She got on his nerves.

He disliked to have her serve him because of the nervous way her eyes blinked, and that made him nervous. He disliked the pale way her hair had of straggling out from under the crisp bows that Selene had contrived for her. In fact, nothing much that Annie could do

[33]

pleased John Lester. Selene knew that and had a way of trying to cover up Annie's short-comings.

"Tell that girl to stop rattling those infernal dishes out there."

"You cannot wash dishes as if they are made out of rubber, John. I'll close the door. The shortcoming really lies in this dinky apartment, you know. All of the rooms are on top of each other."

"Selene, if you don't mind I wish you would serve the dinner yourself. That creature gets on my nerves, with her weak-wristed way of passing things."

"Of course, dear, if you prefer it. You cannot expect trained service, you know, for what you are able to pay for help."

"S'pose not, but you don't have to have a half-wit around."

"She's not a half-wit. A slow-minded creature, I'll admit, but she adores Joan, and that by itself is worth every cent of the paltry wages we are able to pay her."

"Well, she would never be my choice."

"Neither would she be mine, if I could afford to be choosy. Besides, John, you know what we have always agreed. You run your office to suit yourself, and I'll run my house the same way."

"Sure. Sure. But that woman is not competent."

"Well, I am, John, when it comes to running my house."

"You dear, you are that. How did you manage that coat, Selene? It looks like fur. Isn't, is it?"

"No, silly. It's plush caracul. Four dollars and ninety-five cents a yard, and thirty-one dollars and a half complete, with Miss Ada in the house two days to help me make it."

"You're a dear girl, Selene. And some day I'm going to be able to give you the genuine thing."

"You aren't angry with me any more about those amber goblets, are you, sweetheart? I didn't dream of buying them, John, when I first went into the place. The day before the auction, when I saw them in the show-room, I just stood and looked at them for the pleasure one gets out of looking at beautiful objects. I never dreamed that they would be knocked down for a penny under two hundred a dozen. And when I saw them actually going at thirty-six, why, John, I — you wouldn't want me to have been able to resist them. I could sell them to-morrow for two hundred. You aren't angry with me any more, sweetheart? Please say you aren't."

[35]

"You know I aren't, Selene," said John Lester, holding her close, and his dark eyes clouding up with the passion of his love for her. "But try to be good, dearest. And be careful of the tyranny of things. And don't run around to auction rooms, sweetheart. I don't like it."

"You darling. You dear old darling. And now, John, that we have the goblets and those lovely Wedgwood plates I picked up that time at the Madison sale, guess what?"

"Those what?"

"Goosie darling. You haven't even noticed them. Those gorgeous eggshell plates with the grape-and-vine design, that sometimes, when you're very good, I give you your Sunday dinner on. Now that we have them, and the Venetian goblets, guess what?"

"All right — guess what?"

"No, really truly, guess what, darling."

"We're going to have fried apples for supper on them."

"Stop being silly. Guess."

"Can't."

"We're going to have a dinner-party."

"A what?"

"A formal, seven-thirty, floral-centrepiece, creamed-oysters-in-cases dinner-party. Extra-dry in amber goblets, salted almonds, squab

chicken in my darling little Brittany-ware cas-
seroles, and a Nesselrode pudding under pink
whipped cream, that looks like Sherry's and is
made in the Herrick kitchen for the munificent
sum of sixty-five cents."

"That's fine. And whom are you going to
ask?"

"Guess that."

"Mother and the boys from Peekskill and
perhaps——"

"Silly. Want to know? Well, lean close and
— stop teasing, dear — ouch, you hurt my ear
— now, I'll tell you. There — how's that?"

"Why, Selene, you're talking nonsense."

That straight look was out in John Lester's
brow as he withdrew his ear from the pink
warmth of Selene's whispering lips. The
straight look with which he met issues, from
Annie's incompetence on up to decisions which
in later life were to determine issues of state.

"Why am I talking nonsense? Judge Rhincoop is frankly interested in you — is propos-
ing you for his club. Herbert Wing goes out of
his way to invite you to sit at his table. What
is more natural than to invite the Rhincoops
and the Wings here to dinner? Wives and all."

"I'm not on a social basis with those people.
Don't want to be."

"Ah, but, John, I want you to be."

"Haven't the facilities, can't afford them, and don't intend to put up a false front."

"You don't have to, John! Those men will think more of you for letting them see you in your own natural environment. An environment, dear, that you needn't be ashamed of, simple as it is. I've seen to that."

"I'm not a social climber."

"I'm every kind of a climber — for you."

That was the beginning. It took Selene exactly four months of careful drip-dripping of her idea against the slow immobility of John, to achieve that dinner-party.

It took place in the little apartment in Priscilla Court one snowy, traffic-impeded evening in February.

*

The most difficult part of giving a formal dinner-party, if you had only one servant and that a half-competent one who stood staring into space at the most jammed moments of the procedure of preparation, was not so much the concocting of the foods as the scheming to keep them hot for each course, when you had only a two-burner gas-stove without a warming-oven.

For three days before the occasion of the dinner to the Rhincoops and the Wings, the house of Herrick buzzed with the skilfully directed activities of Selene.

MANNEQUIN

Hearts of baby celery, buds of tiny red-and-white radishes, mammoth olives with almond and pimento hearts, lettuce becoming crisper and crisper in damp-towel wrappings, parsley floating in water, sweet butter in pats the shape of tulips, a precious bottle of very extra dry champagne stacked into a cooling-box arrangement nailed to the kitchen window-sill. And the little refrigerator itself crammed with a white firm-fleshed turkey that had been meticulously selected by Selene with countless proddings and bendings-back of wing and leg, all salted, peppered, rubbed with just a whisper of onion, and ready for the oven.

It was not the major things really, though, like the turkey, that mattered most. Or the wine. Or the artichokes with hollandaise. The trifles were what drove one to frenzy. To remember to telegraph Mother to send down her half-dozen silver grapefruit spoons by brother Ed when he came to town from Peekskill on his Thursdays. To see that Annie remembered the white napkin to be wound around the champagne-bottle with just enough of the magic name of Roget on the label showing. Citron for the turkey-dressing. Place-cards with hand-painted corners. Yellow candles for the two majolica candlesticks sent (without John's knowledge) on approval from

an exclusive importer's shop, and with heart-
ache to be returned the next morning. Almonds. A folded playing-card for beneath the
too short fourth leg of the buffet which rattled
so when Annie walked. An empty Havana
cigar-box to be wheedled from the corner tobac-
conist, in which to pass the four fifty-cent
cigars. Two fresh little powder-puffs for the
dressing-table and an array of assorted hairpins,
not forgetting aluminum ones for Mrs. Rhincoop, said to be grey-haired. Pink colouring
for the whipped cream. Six fresh pansies for the
finger-bowls. There were no pansies in the
window-box, but there was enough of trailing
ivy to use as if it were smilax, in a criss-cross
on the Cluny lace table-cover, and white geranium that could be grouped in a jade-coloured
bowl; and for the very centre there was the
orchid. The orchid that had been tended and
saved for an occasion worthy of the slaughter.

Selene was not given to easy tears. Her heart
could hurt with them long before the grey eyes
would dim with them. But the day of the dinner there did occur a trifle around the orchid
that sent the nervous tears in two meanderings
down Selene's cheeks.

For Annie, none too helpful at best except
where her meticulous care of Joan was concerned, actually to impede things with what

amounted to a slow-witted kind of impertinence on, of all days, this crucial one of the dinner-party!

Poor Selene, all tucked up in an apron that
enveloped her, a smear of pink whipped cream
across her cheek and in the very act of snipping
the orchid, when, with a cry that startled her
so that the shears fell clattering to the floor,
barely escaping her foot, Annie jerked her arm
away.

"No. No. You mustn't! The flower.
Please, not that!

"Oh, how you frightened me! You! You
horrid girl. How dare you startle me like that!
Pick up that scissors. Oh, you — how dare
you!" cried Selene, her nervousness and rage
forming the immediate sting of tears across her
eyes. "Didn't I tell you to stay out in the
kitchen and baste the turkey? Is there no way
to make you understand to do what you are
told?"

"The flower, Mrs. Herrick — the — what-
you-may-call-it. The — the ——"

"You mean the orchid? You stupid girl.
Leave go my arm!"

"Don't cut it, Mrs. Herrick. You said —
how it kept itself beautiful — thataway, even
in the window-box. The pretty thing —
shoulda been in a hot-house. Growing in the

little window-box thataway, when it should be under glass ——''

Of course Selene did remember explaining that to Annie, who had a pale way of puttering in among the green and growing edges of the window-box, and who was for ever hovering on the edge of conversations in which, often, she explained to friends the phenomenon of the amusing persistence of the exotic bloom.

"Don't be ridiculous, Annie. I'm cutting the orchid for the centre of the dinner-table this evening."

Annoying silly girl, sniveling actual tears as the shears bit across the stem. As if the day were not sufficient strain unto itself, without the additional ado of Annie, by that jerking of her arm and the cry, frightening her into a state of nerves that later caused her to break one of the six Venetian finger-bowls.

But, withal, the occasion was a success.

Even John Lester, who had groaned so at the prospect, had to admit that. Herbert Wing, a great shaggy personality of a man who completely filled the little living-room, had openly treated his hostess in a delightfully flirtatious manner that no man had since her marriage.

She liked it. Not with anything except her amusement, but just the same it gave her a thrill all down her pretty back where it flowed

into low-cut black satin. She wanted John
Lester in turn to be a little light and flirtatious with Mrs. Wing, instead of just sitting
there refilling the old judge's wine-glass and
absolutely at his heavy worst when one or another of the two women addressed him.

John Lester had no small talk. Selene
writhed at the spectacle of seeing him sit there
so gawkily between gentle old Mrs. Rhincoop
and the quite lovely Greta Wing. She wanted
him to show off. At least to have these women
see him at his clever best. John, who could
talk so passionately and brilliantly when there
was no one to hear except her and the four
walls, on social, scientific, political, and lit-
erary issues of the day, absolutely lustreless
now, between a gentle old lady who wanted to
be benign to him and the brittle and clever
Greta Wing, who was willing to exert herself
to be interesting should the occasion warrant.

Why, the judge, a man well past sixty-five,
could be jovial and, as the wine mounted,
even a little noisy. He had twice Herrick's
youth of manner. And here was Wing, not
one whit cleverer than John Lester, but twice
as suave.

Well, at least from her own angle, the dinner
was a success. There was a hired waitress for the
occasion. The turkey came with creamy folds

of its own slicings stacked temptingly against its flank. The citron-chestnut dressing was commented upon. The Judge cracked his celery noisily as if revelling in its crispness. Sweet potatoes, thanks to a trick of Selene's, came in looking like frothy bananas; and the dessert rose grandly to its peak of pink whipped cream.

Wing, who lived in a fine old house in Gramercy Park, admired in mild, well-mannered surprise Selene's bits of really good pieces here and there. Her carved credenza. A strip of narrow old Spanish velvet. A modern but fairly good triptych done in thirteenth-century manner. He scrutinized a pair of polychrome candlesticks and promised to send her his art-catalogue of the contents of the Davanzati Palace in Florence. And, more than that, in the presence of Lester congratulated her upon the bit of Flemish tapestry, and upon the taste and fastidiousness of their tiny home in general.

The kind of background, Selene knew, John needed to set him off to best advantage before these two men who believed in him. His most important colleagues. The colleagues who could, if they would, conspire toward John Lester's ultimate big achievements.

And at eight-thirty, just as she had planned it, in came Annie, impeccably uniformed, and bearing in the heart of a large lace pillow the baby Joan.

Lovely crowing Joan, her little pink feet bare and kicking to be off the pillow and on their perilous journey about the room, and the gleam of that small perfect body of hers, of which Selene was so secretly proud, faint and rosy through the nightdress.

A great crowing beautiful girl, well able to walk and too large to be held easily in any kind of clutch save Annie's proud and eager one. It was delightful and ridiculous to see the old judge make long skewering sounds in his throat and jibe with his forefinger into the lovely little plumpness of Joan. And Joan, plunging from her pillow and making outrageous advances to Wing with her outstretched arms and somewhat reiterative vocabulary, and wanting to explore the lacy fichu of little old Mrs. Rhincoop, and to reach for the dangle of the long jade earrings which were always part of Greta Wing's effective make-up.

All in all, when Selene closed her tired eyes that night, after the last dish was wiped and the last goblet polished and on its shelf, except for the fact that she was too exhausted to stay awake for it, she was well entitled to the sweet satisfaction of success.

MANNEQUIN

The greediness of Annie. It was like a sea, lapping at her. Threatening to submerge her. And John Lester and Selene were harbouring this greed without knowing it. Were surrounded by it. Menaced by it.

Annie sitting in her little cubby-hole of a room, while John Lester and Selene enjoyed their good-night romp with Joan, eaten as if something were gnawing a hole in her heart. Eaten with greed. The greed over which she seemed to have no control. The greed which was consuming her. The greed for little Joan.

Sometimes, it seemed to Annie, the pain of that was simply not to be borne.

Selene Herrick, who had everything. Annie, who had nothing, sitting in her room with her arms that were empty lying in her lap. Empty of Joan.

It needed all that she could muster in the way of sufficient volition to walk into that front room evenings to surrender little Joan to her parents.

It needed sometimes more than she could muster without an effort of the will that was positively terrifying, to tilt the wheels of Joan's perambulator homeward at precisely five o'clock, according to her mistress's order.

Selene, who had everything, in there on the floor of her sitting-room beside her husband,

romping with her baby. Annie, who had nothing, sitting there regarding the empty cradle of
her arms with the greed — the terrible, irrepressible, lapping greed — and crooning to an
empty pair of arms.

Sometimes in the dead of night Annie, who
slept on an iron cot that was slightly wider
than half of the room she inhabited, would
start up in the dark with this sense of the emp-
tiness of her arms.

Once, when she cried out in the nightmare of
the hurting of the greed, Selene heard, and
asked her the next day about the calling sounds
she sometimes made in her sleep.

The calling sounds that Annie sometimes
made in her sleep were the sounds of greed for
Joan. The sound of a starveling bleating for
sensation. For gratification. And so, night
after night, lying there in the security of their
spick-and-span little home, sharing the very
roof they gave her, lay Annie Pogany, whose
slumber was fitful with her greed for the most
priceless possession of the Herrick household.

And about as close as this knowledge ever
came to percolating through the languid intuition of those immediately concerned was on the
occasions when John Lester made to his wife
some such comment as this:

"Tell that girl to stop kissing the baby. I

don't like it." Or: "Well, she may adore the child, but take my word for it, there is nobody much at home, up where she does her thinking." Or: "If you would spend less time bargain-hunting and more with your child, instead of leaving her with that half-wit, the entire household would be better off."

The kind of remonstrance, however, too casual to make its dent.

As she herself put it, Selene knew a good thing when she had it. In most ways, as servants go, Annie was thoroughly incompetent. Could not so much as broil a chop fastidiously. Or even make a bed so that the sheets were smooth. And certainly she could not wait on table. But you cannot have everything; and, over and above all, Annie was good to Joan. Adoring and adored by her. That left the afternoons to Selene, who so loved to shop and bargain, free for the adventure of browsing into remote side-street shops and auction rooms, where just to wander and speculate as to the ultimate price and ownership of the art objects on display was a better and certainly a less expensive pastime than matinée.

*

And yet it was this allegedly harmless pastime of the afternoon browsings that ultimately was to precipitate a crisis in the Herrick household. The kind of crisis that for the rest of her days was to leave a scar across the heart of Selene Herrick.

Long after the happening was buried in years and the hair of both of them had whitened, that little shirred place of an old wound remained across Selene's heart. A healed scar. But none the less a scar.

Selene could no more have helped coveting that scarf. The scarf that precipitated the crisis. It hung in the exhibition rooms of the Art Auction Galleries in East Fifty-fourth Street. A scarf about a yard square, edged in fringe more than half its width. An arresting Chinese scarf of about the red of berry-stain, which might have been used to make its dye. But what actually made it arresting was that behind the cluster of berries was embroidered the flash of the wings of two great Ho-Ho birds. You caught the tips of the beaks, the curves of claws, and the dash of colour more than you did any definite contours.

It was extraordinary, this illusion of perspective created by mere embroidery. It was the kind of piece which covetous Selene, had she even dared to think in terms of owning it, would have loved for a table-throw, or, better still, to toss lightly across the foot of little

Joan's perambulator as the days became milder and the astrakhan cumbersome.

Rare square of old Chinese embroidery. 32 inches by 32 inches, read the catalogue. Ming period. Mulberry and flamingo shades against mulberry background. Double knotted silk fringe, modern.

It was a piece that would probably bring in hundreds of dollars.

It was a piece to covet just for the bitter-sweet ache of wanting beauty.

But in the end, at the auction on the following afternoon, it did not bring in hundreds. Strangely enough, on probably just the fluke of this or that circumstance, the auctioneer's gavel faltered at ninety dollars. Hung there. Reiterated there. Paused. Importuned. "Going — going — at the ridiculous price of ninety dollars ——"

Selene, sitting there in quiescent mood of mere spectator, suddenly jammed her finger-nails into her palms, as if she would apply the brakes of self-restraint.

"Going — going — at ninety dollars — ladies and gentlemen, do you realize what is happening under your very eyes? This superb piece of Chinese embroidery — of the same rare period of the most famous Chinese porcelains — a Ming piece — priceless beauty — only one of its kind — out of the collection of the late Lord Redingote, Grosvenor Square, London. A piece for the connoisseur. A piece for a museum. A piece to illuminate any home. Throw it over your piano. Hang it on your wall. What am I bid? What am I bid? Going, ladies and gentlemen, at the absurd price of ninety dollars. Who is there here with enough good judgment to capture the prize fabric of this collection? Going — going — at ninety dollars ——"

And then Selene, with her lips stiff, bidding there on the outside of herself. Somebody over whom she had no control, bidding in a light clear voice that came firmly.

"One hundred."

It was incredible. This thing, this precious mellowed antique work of beauty, falling into her hands for the sum of one hundred dollars. Even the auctioneer, on the fall of his gavel, familiar with her pretty face and her sometimes wee and timorous biddings, threw her a look and a smile. "You got a bargain there!"

It took away the edge of panic to her paying down an eighteen-dollar deposit, all she had in her purse, and hurrying home on the street-car, the package that contained the scarf jammed up closely under her arm.

There was no end to the things you could

think up to do with it. It lay over the top of the piano and lit up the room. It hung with exactly the right proportion and colour between the dining-room windows. It fitted precisely into a clumsy niche in the foyer that had bothered her so.

And now, with spring making the astrakhan cover for Joan a bit cumbersome, it lay across the perambulator in just the rich magentas that brought the bird's-wing black out in Joan's hair and eyes and lit up the pallor of her skin.

Poor Annie, who was starting out for the Mall with her charge. There was no getting the thing away from her, once she beheld how it enhanced little Joan.

Her march down the street toward the park was her usual triumphant one, plus. From her high window, peering down at them, Selene could see the passers-by stare, pause, and turn to pet.

Long after Annie and the perambulator were just specks in the distance, the colour of the scarf persisted. A dot of magenta.

*

Of course there was a feeling of scare at the pit of her.

It meant asking John Lester for eighty-two

dollars to pay for a scarf that by no possible manipulation of his kind of imagination could seem to be more than a second-hand shawl.

Selene knew that. Sometimes when they strolled together down Fifth Avenue on mild evenings, it was impossible to get him to pause with her before the windows of jade and chalcedony, fabrics, or rare old murals. He just walked on ahead, so that she had to run to catch up with him.

But by the time John Lester came home from his office that evening of the day of the purchase of the scarf, Selene was quite ready for him. She had worked it all out. Her method of attack. The way to take the edge, right in the very beginning, off what was rather frighteningly certain to be an explosion of wrath, was to begin something like this, with what were sure to be these results:

"John dear, I made some money to-day."

"Who put such ridiculous ideas into your dear little head as the need to make money?"

"Well, just the same, I did."

"How?"

"Bought something."

"That sounds like spending money."

"Nope. Bought something for one hundred dollars and can sell it to-morrow, if I've a mind to, for at least two hundred."

[53]

"That's fine, you little business man, you. But whatever it is you bought, you keep. We're not buying and selling merchandise yet!"

That is the way she had worked it all out. But this is the way it actually happened:

To begin with, as John Lester explained the incredible happening to himself afterward, he had come home with a headache.

He had them sometimes, in bands of steel across his eyes.

It had been a day of panelling jurors, too, a procedure that was always to be tedious and nerve-racking to him.

And then, too, eighty dollars on the eleventh day of the month, when he was in the habit of clearing up all bills on the tenth, was a matter of more moment than it might have been on almost any other date.

Anyway, those were some of John Lester's attempts at later justification of the thing that happened.

"John Lester," cried Selene, in tones that sounded rehearsed even to herself, and perched herself on his chair in a way that jarred his headache, "what do you think?"

"I'm pretty much too all-in to think, dear."

"I made some money to-day."

"Sounds to me like another way of saying I spent some money to-day."

"Why do you say that?"

"Oh, I don't know. A woman's brain can work that way sometimes. But go on — put me right if I'm wrong."

"Oh, you — you take the joy out of everything."

"Why do you say that, dear? If you made some money to-day, without a string tied to it somehow, let us hear about it."

"I did buy something, dear, but ——"

John (drily): I thought so.

Selene: Of course, if you won't let me go on ——

John: Go on . . .

Selene (in a rush of words): I bought a rare antique scarf of the Ming period — same as the porcelain period — for Joan's coach. The child will take cold these warm days with that heavy astrakhan one. I can sell it back to-morrow for twice what I paid for it. The — auction man said so. It's just one of those things that can happen sometimes. Luck. Knocked down to me for a song. One hundred dollars. I paid eighteen down, John, out of — the — the household money I happend to have in my purse. Promised to send the cheque for the rest by mail to-night — and they let me bring it home with me. Can sell it back any time for twice what I paid for it. Pays in the end to buy the best — even the auctioneer congratulated me ——"

Poor Selene. The words began to sound a little silly, but she kept repeating them because the thing that was happening to John was something she could not have foreseen. Nor could he.

John Lester was seeing red. Literally. As he explained it to himself in the tortured hours afterward, red disks were spinning before his eyes. The headache, no doubt, and the depleted feeling of a man who has just met all of his too, too numerous monthly bills.

"By heaven," cried John, and leaped to his feet, trying to sort of grope out for the blur of Selene through the dance of the red disks, "you've gone and spent a hundred-dollar bill for another rag! For a smear of a thing. Well, by God, you have, have you? Go get it, then. Quick!"

"John — John — stop looking that way!"

"Go get it! you hear me. Get that scarf!"

"It's — not here ——"

"Where is it, then? Go get it. I want that rag."

"It's out with Joan on her perambulator."

"It is, is it? Well, when it comes back I'm

going to wash your face with it, to teach you that what you have bought is a piece of rag that is soaked with my flesh and blood. You hear me. I borrowed two hundred dollars to tide me over this month's bills and still have a little margin of it in the bank. If I have to plunk down eighty-two dollars to-night for one of the pieces of rag you would barter your soul for — and mine — there goes that margin. That borrowed margin. Now bear this in mind. When that rag of a thing comes home, I am going to take it and wrap it around and around and around you so that you can see how it feels to be gagged by things — gagged by things — as I am — as I am ——''

Why — it was too horrible. It was too incredible. John Lester, the slow one, like a wild beast there. It was too horrible. It was too incredible.

''How dare you! How dare you — talk to me like this!''

''How dare I! How dare you? You're grinding me down. You've got your heel in my neck. I can't do my work by day, for scheming by night to pay up for you. I paid two hundred and twenty dollars in bills yesterday. Your bills. When I had exactly three hundred dollars in the bank in all. How do you think a man with a family and responsibility and a balance of eighty dollars in the bank feels? Two dollars less than I've got to sweat out for you to-night."

"John ——"

"And now you've thrown away that last borrowed eighty. No man can hope to succeed who is tied to a money-sieve like you. You'll make a grind out of me. You'll take away my future — our future ——"

"How dare you ——"

"Yes, how dare I? A man will dare anything when he is crazy with disgust. With fear. With debt. Why don't you stay at home and run your household like a self-respecting woman whose husband has a future if he is given half a chance? Why, eh? Why? Instead of sitting around auction rooms all day. Loafing around merchandise like any old second-hand junk-dealer."

"Don't you dare — don't you dare to call me — that."

"How do you think it feels for a man to know that all afternoon his wife is around town rubbing shoulders with the junk-dealers? Bleeding him down to the last cent in her mania for things. Things. I'll throw that eighty dollars to the dogs before I'll encourage such performances in my house. Your place is in the home watching over your child. Not gadding the junk-shops. I won't have it. You hear! I won't have it. This let-you-run-your-house-your-own-way agreement is all right so far as it goes. But it doesn't go. From now on you are going to run it my way or not at all."

The boiling and the swirling within Selene. If she could have beheld her face she would have been aghast at it. There was something blanched and strained and dead about it. And her eyes. They came out like two grapes — round, frosted, glazed-looking grapes. And when she struggled for words her lips were two wooden planks, splintery and stiff.

"Well, then, John Lester, what you have said to me this afternoon — the things you have said to me — never — m-my dying day — all my strugglings — am-ambitions f-for you — efforts — make two ends meet — our b-baby — devotion — sacrifice — drudgery. Dinner — scrimp — Rhincoops — Wings — well now, John Lester, if you think you can run this — this house b-better than I — if I'm not fit for — for what you consider the magnificent rôle of your wife — I'm going home. I'm g-going back to mama. I'm going to where I don't have to stand the abuse of a h-husband who is too stingy to buy a perambulator-cover to keep his ch-child warm — I mean cool — I am going to let you run your house and your baby your way. If your nurse-girl doesn't suit you, I'm going to let you afford a better one. Here is where you are going to have a chance to prove your theories. There is cold lamb in the ice-box. And milk. I'm going home and leave you to run your establishment and everyone in it your way."

"Yah — and it will be a darn sight better than the way it has been run, in odd moments from the junk-shops," shouted John Lester, completely beyond self-control now, and banged out of the apartment until the windows, with sunset-glow against them, rattled, and the pewter mugs on the plate-rack in the dining-room rattled also, and Selene's teeth, of sick, nerve-racking frenzy.

*

In the light of that same sunset that lay against the Herrick windows as they rattled, sat Annie in the Mall. One of those heliotrope sunsets of early April that wash a glow over everything. There lay Joan in her coach, sleeping, the clear light on her clear face.

For more than an hour Annie had sat looking at that face with eyes that felt riveted, as if the yearning in them had created some sort of suction. To take her eyes away from Joan was like tearing something. Like tearing flesh.

MANNEQUIN

Poor strange Annie. Coveting Joan. Not wanting to take her back home. Staving off five o'clock. Dreading that surrender of her to the young pair who would be waiting for her in the living-room. Sometimes the bitterness, the bitterness of that impending surrender, welled into a tight knot that became a lump in her chest when she breathed.

It had never been so difficult before. Sitting there looking at Joan asleep, it was as if the little waves, the little lapping waves of the greed, were rising higher and higher about her. Rising into a tidal wave that presently must crash.

Annie coveting Joan. The nights and the days of it. The waking to that sense of empty arms. Night after night of sitting in her cub-by-hole to the sound of the young pair and their offspring, romping. . . .

The nights of it. The days of it. Growing in her. Welling in her. Tightening into that knot in her chest.

That was the day Selene, with valise in her hand, came to the Mall in a quick, nervous kind of flurry that made her seem much younger than her more usual calm and even demeanour.

Mrs. Herrick had been called away. Home to her mother for a few days. Endless admonitions. Unnecessary reiterations about Joan that wearied Annie because she knew them so well. Orders were to come from Mr. Herrick. Then more of the wearying admonitions about Joan. As if caring for Joan were not the most important factor in every day.

The colony of the nurses stared a little at the spectacle of Selene kissing her baby awake. It made Annie resentful, too. Kissing Joan so that finally the child snuggled her face flat down into her pillows for the uninterrupted luxury of sleep. It made Annie fidget with nervousness until the adieus were completed.

Finally Mrs. Herrick was gone. The mother of little Joan was gone, and for days. The mother of little Joan was gone. Suddenly, terribly, it seemed to Annie, sitting there while one after another of the nurse-maids turned their charges homeward, that this time — this time — she simply could not. Now, if ever, was the moment.

Little Joan, hers for the moment, as she lay asleep. So strangely hers to-night of all nights. It lay beyond her power to surrender her this night. The greed and the covetousness out in poor Annie. Mrs. Herrick was gone. She sat there beginning to be sly with that new knowledge. Beginning to be a little terrible with it.

Five o'clock. And Annie, after all the months of the secret coveting, suddenly too greedy to rise from her bench and, in obedience to the annoyingly reiterated orders of Mrs. Herrick, wheel homeward to her father the child there asleep in her charge.

The furtive languid mind of Annie at work. Annie, who had no actual needs. Only the abstract need of the something — the something like the hand of this child — to lay close to the hurt in her heart.

There was the accumulated wage of seven months tied in one of Mrs. Herrick's old silk stockings down in a petticoat pocket beneath the black sateen uniform. There were places — Annie knew them all right — where one could live, remote, away, and safely, with the rare preciousness of Joan.

The coveting was like a pain. It cut her. The coveting and the opportunity! Annie, starveling, wanting Joan for her very own. The rising of the tidal wave of all the months of the lapping waves of the greed. Somehow, suddenly, it became impossible to go home. To him. To Mr. Herrick, waiting to take Joan from her. The little Joan. The lovely Joan.

Annie wanted to sleep with her that night — all night — every night — alone, close, hugged there to the pain in her breast, that would be no pain then.

MANNEQUIN

How did one get the courage? If one took what one coveted, there were the iron-barred windows and the reform schools and the terrible uniforms of the brass buttons. Annie knew — from the old barge days. But if one were wise and sly — how did one get the courage to be wise and sly?

How did one get the courage?

Sitting there in the westering light, Annie Pogany closed her eyes. One got the courage — no special way — one just got it — by chance —— If — oh, say if the next automobile that passed should happen to be red, then that would give one the courage. Chance. Suppose just for fun the next automobile that passes is red. That would give one the courage. That would prove it was all right to take Joan. Mrs. Herrick, who had so much. Annie, who had nothing. Mrs. Herrick was away. Now, if ever! Now or never! Suppose the next automobile that passes is red! If God wants me to do it, the next automobile will be red! That would give me the courage not to go back home with her.

Annie Pogany sitting there with her eyes squeezed, and fearful to open them. If the next automobile is red ——

And opened them to the whiz of a long low red one sliding by.

MANNEQUIN

It was a simple matter of almost calm decision, then, to lift the sleeping Joan from the nest of her pillows, wrap her tightly in the magenta scarf that trailed fringe, and, with the small warm body clutched to the hurt in her breast, wheel the perambulator into a bush and turn in the opposite direction from the home of the Herricks.

*

For three days of pain that had dulled and depleted him, John Lester, torn between the impulse to rush to the railroad station and the determination to hold out as long as possible, tramped up and down his neglected office when he was not tramping up and down his neglected home.

Outrageous, unsuspected streaks of tenacity in this woman he had thought he called his own enough to know her every quirk and folly.

Sometimes, in spite of himself, pacing up and down his incredibly empty living-room, heartsick with remorse and yearning, something like a smile did flit across John Lester's stolid face. After all, the adorable nonsense and pluck of her!

But only for an instant. John Lester wanted his wife. And John Lester wanted his child. And there his anger flared again. How could Selene drag that child on the draughty train ride to Peekskill! He knew, too, the tendency of his mother-in-law to overfeed the youngster. Almost invariably she returned sick from a visit to her grandmother.

After all, if Selene held out one day longer he would swallow his pride and go after her and the baby. The insolent darling. The extravagant reckless unthinking little baggage. Adorable outrageousness. Well, the day would come when he could afford to indulge her weaknesses. Again the flit of smile. And then again the despondency of despair. John Lester Herrick, homesick, and heart-sick.

*

Poor Selene. She hated the house in Peekskill. She had hated it as a child. Outlandish wooden affair with a tower that jutted off on one end like a blister and ruffles of mill-work for trimming. The damp mouldy interior of that house was all cluttered up. With years upon years of her mother's nervous habit of constantly, constantly talking. And the damp and mouldy interior of that house was filled with a definite, tangible smell, inseparable from it. The smell of the pipefuls upon pipefuls of silence that her father, up to the day of his death, had smoked into the chattering.

These three days there with her mother.

MANNEQUIN

The chatter. The chatter. The chatter. Her brothers, who came home from the garage which they ran in partnership in Peekskill, for twelve-o'clock dinner and six-o'clock supper, ate their way silently through it, as had their father before them. The chatter. Eager chatter, innocent of Selene's tragedy of tempest in a teacup.

Selene could no more have brought herself to confide the humiliating fact to her mother that this was any more than a usual pleasure weekend. Selene, whose brain was bursting with wanting to think — wanting to think her way out — submerged in three days of the chatter and chatter.

It was not only John Lester, although her heart was dreary as a moor for him; but hour after hour, and with a gnawing that was actually physical, Selene was wanting her baby. Of course it was worth it, teaching John his lesson in this fashion. Grinding into him a consciousness of the meticulous harassed routine of housekeeping and baby-rearing that he took all too lightly.

Leave it to John Lester, Selene kept repeating under her anxiety, not to neglect the baby; and Annie, in her adoring but poor and foggy way, would help. The real worry was that John and Annie between them might be all too apt to sicken the child with over-attention.

But what if — what if Joan should lie in a draught or fall out of bed, or Annie forget to turn off the electric iron, or John leave his bath-water to run over, or — the what-if's! For the three days of her exile they maddened Selene. They beat up about her like a cloud of bees. The what-if's. What-if!

It was difficult holding out against the pain in her heart for her husband and baby. So difficult that on the third day, and to the buzzing of the what-if's, all of her pride went out suddenly like a lamp. Selene was wanting John Lester. Wanting to feel her cheek against his rough coat. Wanting to sob out to him all the remorseful hurting things that her pride held back. And Selene was wanting her baby. By the end of the third day she could have crawled the fifty miles to her baby.

When Selene walked into their apartment that evening, John Lester, in a kitchen that was littered with dishes with egg-crusts on them, was standing looking out of the window over the waves of the roofs, tugging at his under lip in a fashion he had when nervous.

Of all things that John Lester might have been doing upon her return, the sight of him there, tugging at his nervous lower lip, with one of her checkered bungalow-aprons ridiculously tied about his waist, was the one thing more than she could bear.

Selene, in her relief to be home, burst in upon him, sobbed in upon him in a long coughing sound of hysteria, fearful all the while that Joan was probably asleep and sure to be awakened, but unable to control the long sobs.

"My dearest," said John Lester, and held her to him, and kissed her hair, and kissed deep into her eyes as if nothing short of kissing them all the way in would satisfy. "My dearest," was all John kept saying, kissing her, holding her, embracing her as if he could never let go. "My dearest. My dearest."

She loved to kiss his eyes too, because they were wet. She loved that wetness.

"John. John. John. No matter what comes, nothing can change things between us. Ever. Ever. Ever."

"Nothing, my dearest. Nothing. Ever. Ever. Ever. My dearest. Nothing matters except that you are home."

The two of them breathless and sobbing. Like children, and yet so unconscious of their childishness.

"I shall never leave you again, John. For an instant."

"I was a pig not to come to you first. I was

[69]

just getting ready to pack my grip. You are the biggest of the two of us, dearest."

"I'm not worthy to kiss the toe of your shoe, John."

"Don't say that, darling. It makes me ashamed. And where is ——"

"And now, where is my baby? Has it been hard, darling? Has she been good? Is she asleep?"

"Why ——"

"I hope you're not letting Annie keep her out in the park this late!"

"Why, Selene, what are you saying? Joan is ——"

"John! My baby — nothing is wrong?"

"Why — why ——"

"Don't look at me like that. I can't stand it. Where is Joan?"

"Why, Selene — I don't take it in. Good God! Don't tell me you haven't had her with you in Peekskill! Selene, where is Joan?"

"John! where is Joan?"

"Selene — good God! — where is Joan?"

"I can't bear it — tell me quick — God — where?"

"I thought you took her."

"I left her here — with you — to — to teach you the lesson. Didn't Annie bring her home from the park that — day? John? John."

"Something terrible has happened. I — haven't seen her since I —— I — took it for granted — with you —— Selene, where is Joan?"

It was then that Selene, with a cry that plunged into the silence, pitched forward on her face, striking her brow on the kitchen range as she went down to unconsciousness.

BOOK II

BOOK II

THE granite jungle.

When Joan was old enough to think in terms of similes it seemed that to her. The Lower East Side of New York, where she spent the next thirteen years of her life.

The granite jungle which camouflages everything that comes in contact with it by changing it to the same grey pallor as its sidewalks and courtyards and brick walls. The colour of poverty. The colour of the women's faces and the babies' bodies and the hair of little girls and the lean flanks of dogs and the yellow of Chinese and the russet of Slavs and the blond of Central Europe all camouflaged to the identical pallor of the asphalt jungle. The colour of poverty. The grey of the tenement.

Almost overnight, in their black slit of a room on the fringe of block where the Italian quarter becomes Chinese, Joan's colouring took on the cunning camouflage of the Lower East Side.

That is to say, dressed in the cotton "crawlers" Annie took care to exchange immediately for the sheer made-by-Selene's-hand lingerie, the grey sucked little Joan in against it.

If you had beheld her playing in a cat-and-can-infested courtyard in a clump of children or hugging to herself an alley kitten, the grey would have been stronger than the faintly luminous quality of Joan was pearly. You would have passed her in the grey.

And Annie, made insolent by this sense of security, dared, even while the newspapers of the old men on stoops and the wrappings that sometimes came around a loaf of bread were still blazing with descriptions and photographs of little Joan, to walk down the block with her.

One more child the colour of the tenement. One more ant in the hill. One more mother and child, grains of sand in the desert. It tucked one in so securely, the camouflage.

Even when the day came that the savings in the old silk stocking tucked down into the petticoat were gone, and Annie, with a charge now to come home to evenings, went out gladly enough to day-work as charwoman, she felt the security of that camouflage.

Joan, despite the pallor and the innate fastidiousness with which she played in dirt day by day and yet was untouched by it, was none the less the colour of the slums. Her calico dresses were. The untrained riot of heavy dark hair was. The thick cotton stockings, those loud badges of squalor, full of holes and the horrid grey-green colour of cheap dyes in cheap cotton.

Joan was sucked into the grey all right. The very first week saw to that. The very first week of changing her clothing and burning the dainty things in a pan under the one-burner gas-stove, so that for days the foul room reeked further of that.

And somehow, bereft of the finery, her fair body immediately crammed into the uniform of the tenement, this child became dearer to Annie. Closer, somehow, as if, with the barrier of fine fabrics down, Joan's flesh became closer to the calibre of Annie's flesh.

She loved to huddle the child, there in the dark mouth of their room, close to her, as if the thick cotton denims of her dresses made her a coarser and somehow a closer possession.

How her face could glow out of that gloom! Annie's. A face lit with a gratification, like the firm round glow of a just-filled lamp. She used to croon to her in those first long weeks before the money gave out. All day, soft-voiced nonsenses, tacked to the fore-and-aft of the only couplet she knew:

MANNEQUIN

Bye, O Baby Bunting,
  Daddy's gone a-hunting.

Indeed, daddy had gone a-hunting.

*

Sly Annie. With all the cunning of the low-geared brain, there was, she realized, the matter of the name to be taken care of.

The name "Annie Pogany" must go. Like the flame of a candle when you douse it. That was easy enough. If you were insolent with a sense of security, your cunning told you that you might even keep the "Annie," as a blind. Annie what? There was nothing to suggest the printed word except the label on a wooden trash-box under the sink.

"Sargossa Brand." Annie what? "Sun-Ripened Tomatoes. Sargossa Brand." Annie Sargossa. That would do.

But the choosing of a pseudonym for Joan was another matter. The days dragged into weeks and the weeks into months during the period that Annie's funds held out, and except when she ventured down the block with the child to the push-cart markets, there she sat, huddled with her most of the days through, Joan held close to the hurt in her breast.

And still Annie could think of no name for Joan. No name sufficiently eloquent of the curious dusky-pearl quality of fairness. And Annie wanted that kind of name for this Possession of hers. None of the few she could think of quite suited. Not Annie. "Miss Lizzie" had been the name of a housekeeper at Redfern Reformatory who had once been kind to her. But somehow "Lizzie" would never do. "Mary" had been the name of one of the girls who had worked alongside her in a hand laundry. A lovely name, but the girl herself horrid with face sores. "Bella" was a name, and "Ida." A Miss Daisy for whom she had once scrubbed floors in a lunch-room used to give her pink mints. But no, not "Daisy." . . .

There was a flower —— Poor slow-geared brain of Annie. It was so hard to remember much of anything. But there was a flower that reminded her of the way her Possession, there in the grime of that room, somehow shone through it, with persistence.

Nothing could seem to quench that luminosity. Neither the thick grey cotton stuffs that clothed her, the dirty wooden floor upon which she played, nor the soot of the tenements. She could wallow with the Italian children of Prince Street, mixed in with a few of the slant-eyed Oriental ones from Mott Street, down in the furiously dirty courtyard, and yet somehow not seem to gather its filth.

Annie's Possession, in a world of children with
grime ground against their faces, kept somehow clear-skinned. The amazing integrity of
her! The persistent fastidiousness in surroundings that were fœtid.

There was a flower ——

Day after day, night after night, when Joan
lay on the pallet beside her, close to the trou-
bled, the puzzled beating of her heart, Annie
lay trying to remember.

There was a flower ——

The one in the window-box in the dining-
room at the Herricks'. A cream-and-mauve-
coloured one that grew out from the homely
box of phlox and geranium.

The exotic thing that did not belong there.
The exotic thing that persisted through.

More than once Annie had heard Mrs. Herrick describing the phenomenon to friends,
and that day of the dinner Mrs. Herrick had
pronounced the name to her angrily and
clearly.

There was a flower — a flower. Week after
week of groping to remember the name. In
a corner hardware store they sold envelopes
of flower-seed. The clerk read the names of
them off to her. Pansies. Verbenas. Phlox.
Nasturtium. No. No. No. Not one was the
name of the flower that kept all of its beauty

there in the green-painted window-box of the Herricks' dining-room.

Annie beating about days and half the nights trying to remember. There was a flower . . . there was a flower. . . .

And then one evening, by the ridiculous analogy of a pork chop she was buying for their meal, the name came to her on a clap of recollection. The *o*-vowel in pork must have done it.

Orchid! That was the name of the flower. That was the name of the flower that for persistent daintiness reminded her more and more of the mauve-and-cream-coloured beauty that was Joan's.

Orchid.

And thus it was that when the time came for the Possession to swap names with the neighbourhood children and to put her signature on application-cards for public school and health certificates, Orchid Sargossa was the hodge-podge appellation of the little girl.

A little girl who, come to think about it, if you had time to single her out of the thousands about her, did have a little something to the tinge of her that was exotic.

*

It is improbable that, even in the squalor of those early days of her little-girlhood, Orchid could have been termed an unhappy child. At any rate, not for the first of them, in that period when Annie was part of an environment that she took to be the entire world.

That was her universe, bounded by Prince Street, Mulberry, and Mott. All children had a Nana like hers, except the Raviollas, whose Nana died and all eleven of the youngsters had "got sent" to the asylums.

Otherwise, all Nanas seemed pretty much the weather-stained, labour-stained women who were none of those things to Orchid, because apparently the law of Prince and Mulberry and Mott Streets was that all Nanas were in that image.

Sometimes, if something revolted in her at her own Nana when she beheld her sloughing about the room barefoot, it was not so much because of any acute consciousness of the sordidness of the spectacle, but rather that it would have gone so against the grain of Orchid's own little pink-soled feet to let them blacken and thicken at the soles as Annie's did, and protrude out of shape in great calloused knobs.

Nana never cared whether Orchid went barefoot or not. But somehow, even in the breathless, reeking July days when most of the children in the tenement lay naked on fire-escapes and down on the bleaching sidewalks, Orchid could never bear to let her flesh come directly in contact with the dirtiness.

The flesh of her young body, in a world of sour unfastidious bodies, she kept firm and cool-feeling by letting the water from the faucet run down over her as if she had been a little marble knoll.

With her instincts she avoided somehow the contacts with the dirtiness. Annie, who used to wash out and rough-dry her little misshapen dresses, did it slovenly, almost seeming to grind the dirt in. Then during the long shut-in days, the lonely days when Nana was out at charwork, she climbed on a chair beside the sink and washed them out all over again. And sometimes a coarse denim sacque of Nana's, to surprise her with when she came home.

Before she was five, she knew the trick of looking out for her tiny self. When the whistles down along the wharves blew noon it was time to drag the chair over to the packing-case that served as table, scratch a match carefully held away from her eyes the way Nana had shown her, and make a flame under the pan of veal-neck stew Annie had left in position on the burner.

Sometimes she went down into the courtyard to shout into the squalor along with the other

children, or on rainy days down into the long
slit of hall that ran through the house like a
tunnel. But once in this hallway, when Orchid was six, a boy said horrid frightening
things to her; things that she did not understand, but that were horrid and frightening to
her none the less. And so, for the most part,
the child remained up in the room all the day
while Nana was gone, or played in the neigh-
boring tenement rooms with little girls of her
own age. Horrible rooms invariably filled
with the bickerings of the tired misshapen
women and too many children, and men who
staggered in often on the sea-legs of drink.

One evening, though, an investigator came
around from the Community House and asked
Nana to send her child to Day Nursery during
those hours when she was forced to be away
from home.

At first Annie, full of private flocks of fears
that darted through her brain, demurred. But
a probation officer from the city courts called
and threatened to take the case in hand, and the
investigator brought to bear a persuasion that
conquered Annie's fears. And so the child,
called for in a yellow omnibus that plucked the
little charges off the kerb-stones, entered a new
life.

It was pleasant at the Day Nursery, braiding

shiny coloured papers into mats and tracing
birds and colouring them red and blue and
green with water-paints.

Poor Nana. Sometimes, evenings, with her
cracked old lye-bitten stumps of fingers, she
used to sew dresses that Orchid might be more
presentable for Day Nursery. Coarse bulbous
things that, because they were new and there-
fore clean, were lovely to the child.

*

Those were years, for Annie, of a poor fogged
kind of fulfillment.

The days-in and days-out of swabbing down
the corridors and lavatories of office buildings
that sometimes overlooked harbour and Statue
of Liberty, were soapy, soaked, scummy affairs, but they led to home and the Possession
who slept with her lovely hand against the
hurt in her heart.

The thawing hurt of the starveling.

For all the years of the Possession's little-
girlhood they slept side by side on the lump
of a pallet they called bed, the child's hand, in
an unconscious and precious habit she had,
spread against the hurting place in Annie's
bosom, as if she would heal it.

Except for the mental dimness of Annie, and
except for a variability of temperament that

made her sometimes broody and even a little vicious if crossed, this woman, in her greedy way, was kind to Orchid.

And, with the delicate tendrils of the easy affection of childhood eager to fasten themselves, Orchid turned her love upon the fragment-minded woman she called Nana and literally danced her way through a murky childhood that, for want of a basis of comparison, was not murky to her.

Inevitably, of course, the lurid patter of the tenement, and some of the patois, found its way to Orchid's lips. But, strangely enough, not to linger there. Before she had even started to public school the counteracting environment of the day nursery had pitted itself against a diction that gradually she was to shed, along with the habits of sucking pennies under her tongue as the children in the courtyards did, and of jerking bits of fruit or pickles off the push-carts when the pedlars' backs were turned and darting into the black mouths of doorways.

Little Orchid, leading the everyday life of the everyday tenement child, except for the persistence of the qualities in her that kept her hair in a smooth black-wing fashion against her clear cheeks, while Annie's, for need of washing, hung lusterless in clumps; and that

kept her mouth somehow as clean and as fresh
as a bud in a bowl, even in the days when she
sucked her pennies as naturally as she filched
fruit off push-carts.

*

Hurdy-gurdy slum days. The relentless panorama of the tenements. The zigzag fire-escape-
cluttered vistas. Open-mouthed ash-cans with
the dust shooting out in quick spirals. Lean-
flanked cats and children. The dance of the
wash-lines. Ever since she could remember,
when she was scarcely tall enough to peer
above the window-sills and later when her
knees were only parallel with them, that was
the vista upon which she opened and closed
her eyes.

The dance of the clothes-lines. Gibbets of
union-suits hanging from them. Waving of
coarse flannel arms. Tossing of balbriggan
legs. Tiny children's dresses impaled at the
shoulders by clothespins. That was the vista;
and the sounds from that vista were the squeal-
ings of the pullings of the pulleys, drawing in
and out. The clothes-lines and the mewlings of
cats and the shoutings of children and the roar
as of the roaring sea, of the Lower East Side.

Sometimes there were neighbourhood pa-
rades and festas of the Italian children on
Prince Street. Once Orchid wore a gilt paper

crown on her head and walked in the public
school parade on Decoration Day.

Annie had snipped out the crown with her
lye-bitten hands and scissors that groaned with
rust. Poor Annie! it should have been ten
minutes' work, cutting out the tiara from the
strips of pasteboard and covering it with gilt
paper furnished by the school. But her hands
were such stubs by now! and so the cutting and
the snipping and the pasting took evenings of
unrelenting labour by gaslight, after the days
of the scrubbing of the corridors and lavatories.

It was fine, though, seeing Orchid march in
the parade, with a staff wound in red, white,
and blue and a gold star at its head, also
snipped out by Annie. Annie, sitting on the
kerb with her skirts only half-way tucked out
of the gutter, kept blinking her eyes and chattering her pride with the tenement mothers.

Pride of possession. Slow-witted Annie, her
face made nervous leaping movements with it.

And once, too, when Orchid was eleven,
slowly and laboriously, out of a whole week of
evenings, Annie had fashioned her, out of pink
tissue paper, a Queen-of-the-May dress.

Orchid was to be Queen of the May at the
public school celebration, and to walk under a
pink paper canopy held up by her classmates,
and to recite, while a chorus of fifty fifth-grade

[88]

children chanted after, The Battle Hymn of the Republic.

It was terrible to see Annie's stubs of fingers puttering among the frail tissues. Orchid, only eleven, wanted to wrap and drape the bright stuff herself. And did finally, when Annie was off at charwork, unpleating clumsy folds of tissue until the frock flared from her like a whirl of inverted rose-petals.

Triumphantly, that holiday, Orchid was Queen of the May.

Queen of a few hundred little yearlings like herself, with their coarse hole-peppered stockings showing out under the frail tissues, and the dreary lingerie of the tenements peeping darkly below the pink butterfly shoulder-bows.

The celebration took place one Saturday afternoon, on a dry plot of ground between tenements, that was as parched as an old tongue.

Orchid in the pink tissue caused the rim of mothers and children around the kerb-stone to clap their hands as she came along. Annie, who had taken the half-day off, was among these mothers.

Suddenly, marching along under the pink canopy, it came over Orchid, with the shock of the first self-consciousness on the subject

she had ever experienced, that among the
rather grim frieze of the tenement mothers
along the kerb-stone — even among them —
Nana was somehow the most grotesque. The
most like one of the stone gargoyles' faces
carved above the entrance of the fifty-two-
storey office building where Nana scrubbed.

Thus, when Orchid was barely thirteen,
there was something already of the crone about
Annie Pogany. The clumps of hair. The snag
of front tooth that bit down into her lower lip.
The dim and shifting eyes and the heat-light-
ning manner in which her features jerked. The
nervous twitchings that, as time and the something else wore on, became more and more
noticeable.

The something else.

When it first began to happen, Orchid could
not try to co-ordinate the frightening facts of
it to herself without going off into nervous
paroxysms of crying that made her breathing
jerk for hours afterward.

Once in school, after Annie had been particularly dreadful, one of the fits of crying seized
Orchid so that they were obliged to send her
down into the principal's office, where he and
two teachers worked over her.

But Orchid would no more have revealed her
plight! For years it was as if this child were

literally spreading her meagre skirts to hide a shameful situation that scorched her with a sense of shame.

Orchid would no more have revealed the cause of her nervous collapse! For years, even since she had been seven and had entered the primary grades of public school, Orchid had lied about the Thing. Valiantly. There never was a time, when questioned by the social workers and investigators who made their rounds of the tenements, that Orchid did not lie for Annie. To the investigators. To the neighbours. Even to herself.

What had happened was this: Under the circumstances, the natural thing. The almost-to-be-expected thing.

Annie, so full of desire and with only the ful-fillment of the one Possession, had scrubbed corridors alongside a crone of a woman who opened up to her, on the whiff of one sniff of white powder, whole new realms of sensation that not only equalled, but indeed surpassed, the gratifications she enjoyed through the child.

When Orchid was eight, Annie had already begun to take drugs.

When Orchid was ten, Annie, who, mind you, all her life had been a starveling of re-formatory and institution, and who still had a

[91]

little roundness to her figure and a bit of gilt to her hair, began to realize the devious ways that, if luck was with you, were easier than charwork.

From the time she was eight until she was thirteen, it was as if Orchid were trapped in the vise of an environment that could have destroyed her from almost every side. The dreaded little bottles of white powder that lurked under the mattress and in the pendulum part of the clock. The curious glass tubes that Annie kept concealed in a bit of old lining torn from a hat. Flat bottles with screw tops that protruded from queer hiding-places. The strange shabby and often lurching men who smelled of the sea. Bargemen. Tattooed old sea-dogs. There was a certain freighter that came in every fourth week. Before she quite realized what anything meant, Orchid had learned to estimate and dread the coming of that boat.

There was one who wore his shirt open and had a beard on his chest. He was the one who came to the room the week that the freighter was in harbour. Sometimes then — sometimes then — all the night ——

Those were the things that, even in retrospect, could send Orchid into the terrible, the secret cryings.

Frequently, though, Annie went off. All night. That was better. Except for the fear of lying there alone on the pallet. Thinking the things. Fearing the things.

It was not that she did not love Annie. Poor barren gnarled-looking mother to her. The myth about her father (Annie's myth), who must have been a fine and handsome father, with a waxed-upward moustache, made her sorry for Nana. And for herself. To have lost him as husband. To have lost him as father. Nana had told her about him so often, as they lay there on the pallet. He had been the owner of a barge, a fine one with a red cabin, and one night had gone down with it. Poor Nana. Poor Orchid. Long after Orchid had fallen asleep, Annie, with the child's hand clutched passionately to her, would lie there croaking into the silence. Poor Nana. Poor Orchid.

It was only when she was groggy that this woman who had fostered Orchid, sewn her dresses with poor lye-bitten fingers, and fashioned her pink tissue May frocks when her back jerked with pain, could be alien to her, and even terrible. Terrible with the strange irascibilities of the drugged mind.

Annie, who loved to fondle Orchid, could pinch her arms then so that, for days after one of Annie's "spells," Orchid wore only the long-sleeved of her little dresses in order to hide the black-and-blue marks.

Annie had struck her once, too, across the eyes, in one of these attacks when she was "not well," and broken open the flesh at the top of the bridge of her nose; and for nights after the "spell," which had been a particularly bad one, had dragged herself out of bed three and four times to lay wet cloths upon the ugly gash that kept opening from the riding of the flesh between Orchid's eyes.

And once, when Annie must also have been gin-soaked instead of just cruel and cunning from the powder, she began to yell because Orchid had dropped her slate. No other reason. But she was horrible. Pursuing the child in uncertain careening steps from corner to corner of the room.

Orchid dreaded most, though, the loud-breathing longshoremen. The men with stubbles of beards and eyes with red threads in them.

Their eyes slid over her so, giving her almost the horrible feeling of awakening, as one frequently did in the tenement, to the crawl of a roach.

Sometimes, when she came home from school, the thought smote her: what if she should enter the room and find one of them there, without Nana? The one who wore his shirt open, even in winter, and had the terrible chest. Frequently, when she left for school in the morning, one of them was still there.

It kept her frightened and on edge every time she turned the knob of the door that led to that room. Except that in her heart she knew Nana. Never had she been sufficiently druggy to permit one single one of them, with the sliding eyes that could frighten so, to so much as touch her.

Once a sailor, not one of the young ones with jaunty shaved heads and little white duck caps, that walked Prince Street sometimes, but an old dried prune of a sailor with a quid in his cheek, made a feint of grabbing her by the waist one day as she came in from an evening in the reading-room of the Settlement House.

Why, Annie had leaped at him with a litheness she seemed much too gnarled for. Not one of them who came into that room ever dared to more than let their eyes slide.

They knew somehow, with their intuition. There was growing up unsullied in the horridness of that room, literally, a little orchid.

Annie, even as the fog between her and reality seemed to settle like milk in the watery blue of her eyes, and her perceptions grew duller and duller, saw to that.

Hands off of Orchid.

*

The Settlement House helped.

It meant that she was scarcely at home at all.

Most of the time it was Annie herself who, loving the fragility of her Possession's hands, which, as they grew older, grew longer, slimmer, paler, would not permit Orchid to so much as brew a stew.

Annie did those chores herself evenings, when she came home, smelling of lye and with her hair leaking out of her hat in clumps.

And so, after school in these crowded, busy years before she was ready to enter junior high school, Orchid, rather than come home to the door of a room whose handle she always dreaded to turn for fear of what it might disclose, spent long happy hours at the House.

The house of a thousand doors to the jammed spirit of Orchid. Reading-rooms with window-boxes, cretonne hangings, and painted chairs.

Twice a week a young woman in rimmed spectacles, who came down to the House in a closed car with a cornucopia of fresh roses which the neighbourhood little girls begged from her as she alighted, told stories

in the assembly-room from four until five.
The charmed and glittering stories of Lancelot
and Elaine. Sir Galahad. Jason and the
Golden Fleece. Pandora. Lady of the Lake.
Paul and Virginia. Evangeline. And then:

"The splendour falls on castle walls."

And

"Tweed's fair river broad and deep."

There was something about those lines that
was a sea rolling into melody.

She learned to sew there, too, minute stitches
and firm, straight hems. And evenings from
six to nine-thirty the reading-room was hers,
to roam through the enchanted aisles of pages
of the rich world of lore and fancy, fact and
rhyme.

There was a little Jewish girl named Sadie
Rosalsky, with whom Orchid used to sit, arms
intertwined, poring over their joint selections
from the shelves. Old Curiosity Shop. Golden
Treasury. Short Glimpses into the Classics.
Gulliver's Travels. Tales from Shakespeare.
Idylls of the King. Ingoldsby Legends. An-
cient Mariner.

One day she was sent on an errand by one of
the teachers with a note up to the rooms of
Miss Walter, head of the house. Rubbing her
cotton-ribbed ankles one against the other,

as she stood waiting for a reply, and staring, it was precisely as if something in her had unfolded.

Of warmth. Or recognition. Recognition of things she loved even before she had known they existed. Undreamed-of niceties. Fresh flowers in brass bowls. Firelight that lay in pools in dark wood. A round Chinese teak-wood table with pearl inlay and spread with a yellow tea-set. A velvet couch of old blue that faded pleasantly into the quiet room. Cool-feeling bits of black and white on the wall. Etchings, with wide white mats and narrow black frames.

The first room of nice appointments and nice taste that she had ever seen. It was as if something as vague as the first nerve-twitch of a tooth about to ache, had set in.

Up to this point Orchid's consciousness of the black slit of room she and Nana called home had been little more than a realization that there was something poorer about it and meaner than even the poor and mean tenements about them. But now, suddenly, a brand-new consciousness had lifted its head. She knew with her mind what before she had only sensed. She knew now, standing in that pretty sitting-room, how bitterly she hated ugliness.

*

MANNEQUIN

Then this happened:

If she had been more than just turned fourteen, and, inexplicably enough, a strangely innocent fourteen, she must inevitably have seen it coming. But somehow, because she had reckoned with horridness so long — the horridness of the looks of the longshoremen, the horridness of the little boys she was obliged to pass in the long black tunnel of hallway, the horridness of the street jargon of which she somehow managed to keep her lips clear — there was in her perhaps, unconsciously, a false sense of immunity.

The advances of men upon her prettiness Orchid had learned to resist while she was still lisping. Not-nice little boys to be jabbed with pins that she wore ready for them on the under side of her skirt-belt.

Sadie Rosalsky was the only chum of her little girlhood. She had a father with a great white spade of beard, who sat all day behind the counter of his Kosher butcher-shop chanting and swaying over a magnificent old tome called the Torah.

Sarah hated this "greenhorn" manifestation of her father reading his Torah in public. Somehow, but secretly, because Sadie's indictment of "greenhorn" could be a scathing one, Orchid loved the solemn spectacle of the old man behind his counter, swaying to a rhythm that must have been a rhythm of the spirit. Rhythm. Rhythm of God. . . .

He was like an organ, Sadie's patriarch father there among his sides of beef and chicken-pluckings. A grand old rhythmic person. And Sadie, who had been born in Prince Street and had a sharp, quick, clever little tongue in her head, that jangled like a new tin bell, sharing her father's roof and yet withal a creature of another world. The quick terrific world of a new country amalgamating out of the melting-pot.

But just the same, she was the only one of the neighbourhood girls whose language and thoughts were not mixed with the gutter residuum of the Lower East Side.

Sadie loved to walk up and down the jammed, push-cart-infested sidewalks evening after evening, with her arm about Orchid's waist, and repeat the charmed lore of King Arthur or chant "The splendour falls."

It was a charmed adventure to crawl with quick clever Sadie, whose mind, by heritage, was touched with beauty, into the rhythmic snug harbours of poetry. It matched up with incipient yearnings for rooms with firelight flickering in mahogany and the stern patriarchal beauty of Sadie's swaying father.

MANNEQUIN

There was something about Sadie fierce, oriental, and luscious, like a rich dark plum. There was a certain kind of splendour about Sadie.

Knowing her made the days brighter, and safer from the gutter residuum. That and the knowledge that Nana in her way was keeping guard. And yet there was always the lurking fear. What if Nana, when the milk of the fog was thickest in her eyes — what if Nana did not, might not, know enough to keep guard?

And that is precisely what did happen, one Sunday afternoon after Orchid had left Sadie on the sidewalk below and had dashed upstairs into the room, her healthy young appetite demanding supper.

In the four hours that she had been away, the longshoreman had come. The one with the bare chest, whom she dreaded most. That meant that a certain freighter was in.

He was sprawled out in the only rocking-chair the room possessed, his great feet out in the middle of the floor. Annie, who must have been sitting across the enormous hypotenuse of those thrust-out legs, rose hurriedly as Orchid burst in, and picked up one of the bottles from the litter of them on the floor. Empty bottles that Orchid knew and dreaded by the shape and the odour. Gin-bottles.

And Nana was not herself. Terribly not herself. She careened as she walked; and when she flopped herself down on the pallet and just sat there looking all caved-in and boneless, the hair came down in clumps over her eyes, and the fog in them made them look frighteningly milky and sightless.

Usually, upon occasions like this, Orchid just waited, with the frozen feeling out all over her, for the visitor to shamble himself out of the room and enable her to get Nana to bed.

She knew the whole procedure. The slow business of getting her into the stiff old cotton flannel wrapper she called a nightgown, and helping her, inch by inch, in between the bed-covers. And then Nana, who usually had two or three dollars in bills after these visitations, waking out of her state to cry and moan her promises never to have it happen again.

Life could be consistently nauseous. One could grow accustomed even to horror.

But this day there was something so limp about Nana. So silly. It was her silliness that first smote Orchid with an unusual alarm.

"Nana," she cried, and started toward her for fear she might topple forward on her face and cut her head on the stove-edge as she had been known to do.

Rushing toward Nana like that meant

climbing over the outstretched fling of long-shoreman. That was her mistake. Because, tripping as she took the little leap, her ankle banged against his; and suddenly, in arms that were as terrifying to her as the arms of a gorilla, he had her. Held her. Held her so that the roughness of his chest touched her cheek.

"Nana!" she cried, and struggled, and sank her teeth into his arm. "Nana. Nana." Always keeping her voice under her breath, for that fear of the neighbours, and struggling as she bit, and biting as she struggled. "Nana, Nana, don't let him!"

But Nana, in pallid droop there on the side of the pallet, was too silly to care. Too not herself. Nana, after all the years of the protection, was failing her. "Oh, Nana, Nana." And Nana only sat back and drowsed while she bit and kicked and plunged with her fists against the bare chest that horrified her.

"Let me go. You. You." But in whispers, even while her fear blinded her. "Let me go. You! Or I'll bite and I'll kick. Nana, please, won't you please! Nana! Call him off. Nana!" she cried out; and then on a shriek that slipped up and got beyond her control, "Nana, won't you help?"

His eyes were so close. Pin-wheels that spun.

The eyes that had so often slid over her, but always, while Nana was on guard, passively. Pin-wheels now that spun. And the stubble of him. He was all stubble. Stubble of jowl, of chest, and the backs of his hands. Orchid frantic with terror. Superhuman with terror.

Without knowing how, as he had her there with his close face breathing against hers in two loud streams, in some way with a litheness born of emergency, she was clear of him. And with a low swooping motion, a dodge under his arms, was out, down the stairs, through the black tunnel of hall, out into the blessed security of the slum-swarming street.

She ran. She ran. And there was the sound of sobbing and drowning in her ears. She ran. Trembling and sobbing and choking with silent hysteria by the time she reached the House.

A teacher, passing in the hall, touched her lightly on the head as she hurried past.

"Good evening, Orchid."

"Good evening, Miss Daly," she said through the roaring of the drowning noises in her ears.

Another teacher looked up and smiled as she entered the reading-room.

And Orchid smiled back through the roaring as of drowning.

She took down a book from a shelf. The first

one she laid throbbing eyes on and carried it to a chair beside a window.

First Rudiments of Chemistry: A Handbook.

For two hours, crouched in the attitude of concentration, with unseeing eyes forced against the title-page, she sat there trying to get back composure. Struggling to keep her lips steady. Compelling her eyes to focus until they could make out the letters on the page. Handbook of Chemistry. Stilling the sobbing in her throat and the drowning noises in her ears by the effort of making her fingernails relax from biting into her palms.

Two hours in the casual attitude of reading there, and all the while struggling to relax herself of the horror; and by half-past nine, closing-time — composed enough to hear someone entirely outside herself saying in light natural tones that she recognized as her own:

"Good-night, Miss Daly. Yes'm, it's the first book on chemistry I've ever read. Yes'm. Thank you. Good-night, Miss Turnbell."

*

After spending more than an hour on the landing, listening with her ear to the lock and gathering up her courage to try the knob, Orchid did finally peer in.

The room was empty. There were two more

corkless bottles on the floor beside the rocker, and the overturned stool that she had kicked over as she fled was still on its side.

Nana did not come home that night. Nor the next. Nor the next.

It was the first time she had ever remained away for more than two consecutive days.

By the fifth night the landlord, and then the authorities, got wind of it.

The sixth, Orchid slept on a clean little cot in what was called the infirmary of the House.

The seventh, Miss Walter signed an order on a dotted line, and the machinery of philanthropy was set in motion. The eighth day "Orchid Sargossa. Vagrant parentage" was temporarily entered on what was known as an emergency slip in the Clara von Hutten Vocational School for Girls, in East Sixty-first Street, near what is known as the Fifty-ninth Street Bridge.

And, drab as it was, a five-storey brick building surrounded by warehouses and permeated by the odour of lysol and philanthropy, it was by all odds a vast improvement upon anything she had previously known.

Indeed, except for the transfer picture of the warm room of brasses, cretonnes, and mahogany of Miss Walters, stamped so indelibly against Orchid's brain, the von Hutten Home would have amounted to luxury.

The white iron cot with the coarse clean sheets in a cell of a room all to herself.

The bath at the end of the hall. The tub that she scoured with a brush and a can of gritty stuff, there for the purpose; and then into the gleaming porcelain, and the plunge of clear steaming water into which she stepped with the whole of her body at once. Long, slow luxury of that. And the fresh shaggy bath-towel left every other day on her doorknob. Sometimes, in the deliciousness of the bath, she missed the breakfast-gong and went without her mug of good coffee and choice of soft-boiled egg, gruel, or stewed prunes.

But breakfast did not matter so much as just to lie, even selfishly, with the other girls trying at the knob, and let the flesh relax to the luxury of the bath.

By the first week-end Orchid was enrolled in three evening classes: designing, millinery, and English composition. The week following, in fresh middy-blouse and pleated blue serge skirt from the wardrobe department of the Clara von Hutten, she presented a stamped and printed slip, handed her at the Home, to the Employment Department of the Titanic Department Store on Broadway and Thirty-fourth Street.

MANNEQUIN

One hour later, a strip of navy-blue ribbon around the upper-arm of the middy-blouse, with "Service" embroidered on it in red, Orchid started her career as cash-girl in the Titanic.

To Orchid the Titanic was like some great land-monster that chewed her up day after day, rolled her, masticated her, everything but gulped her, and then spat her out at six o'clock with pretty much all of the juices of life out of her and down into the monster.

At least, the first twelve or fourteen weeks were like that. The backs of her legs hurt so. All of the strength seemed drained out of them at the close of a day. And the white incandescent lights over the aisles made her skin feel their colour. And the din of the Titanic and the din of her heart and the beat of her pulse and the roaring in her ears all day long, all night long, bawled out, "Cash. Cash."

The air of her waking and the air of her sleeping were full of it; the beating of wings together in a noise like "Cash."

"Cash," shouted the silence as she floated off to sleep in her cell of a room.

"Cash," shouted the day coming at her murkily through the windows that looked on to the flank of a warehouse.

Cash. Cash. Cash.

MANNEQUIN

It was difficult, in the din, to miss Nana as acutely as the occasion would seem to have warranted. Except for the ache when she thought of her in such moments as bending with her poor old stubs of fingers over the pink tissues, or sitting with her face in that dreadful-looking gargoyle smile of pride while she danced in the gilt paper crown, the din of the days crowded her out.

Sometimes, alone in the room that was so blessedly clean to her, Orchid did cry herself to sleep, but as much perhaps of mystery as of pain. And yet, underneath it, the ache. Poor Nana.

Nana must have gone off somewhere, with the milk in her eyes befogging them; off somewhere with the — the one who was all stubble. The backs of his hands. His jowl. His chest. Off somewhere, the two of them, befuddled. Accident of dark embankments. Barges that go down at night. . . .

They told Orchid at the station down in Mulberry Street precinct, where she went occasionally long after the case had ceased to be more than a record, that the woman known as Annie Sargossa, her mother, had probably shipped with the seaman described in her room that Sunday afternoon of the disappearance.

Shipped with the seaman. Hardly Nana,

with her eyes all milky and too dull to
care. Dark embankments, rather, water under
bridges. . . .

And then, one day, a patrolman brought in a
travesty of a sailor hat with a lump of cotton
rose against the crown.

It lay for weeks in a litter of objects in the
station, waiting for identification, until Orchid
plucked it gingerly out, on one of her visits of
inquiry.

It was Nana's hat, picked up by the patrolman along a wharf.

*

Suddenly, if none too subtly, came the consciousness of her own beauty. The girls in the
Clara von Hutten told her. They gathered in
her room evenings to watch her brush out the
sleek black wing of hair, and they said that her
complexion was like the cream-coloured plush
that lined the baby coffin in the undertaker's
window on Lexington Avenue.

It was fun being beautiful. It made the girls
defer a little. Orchid had money, now, too.
In sums. Eight dollars a week, four of which
went nominally for room and board, which the
girls in the Clara von Hutten were expected to
pay in proportion to their earnings.

Then there were the four left over, after the
items of the middy-blouse and skirt were paid,

and carfares, umbrella, cold cream, lisle-thread stockings, castile soap, and all the delightful accessories that had, here in this brand-new world, become necessities.

And then, from the accumulated savings of the week, there was enough still left for quite a little row, on the back of the wash-stand, of the cheap daintinesses of soap and scent that one craved; and then still enough left over to venture down into the dressmaking department, where the Clara von Hutten apprentices would make a frock for the amount in one's purse.

After the first weeks of the lassitude from the pain in her back and her legs, the thrill of the growing awareness of her beauty began to mount.

Down in the dressmaking department they gave her samples of dress fabrics and crowded around her in bevies. "That blue serge will make up swell for you." "They're all the cuckoo down at Franklin's this week. Blue serge twills are." "Oh say, that'll be swell made straight silhouette for you, Ork."

Or: "Here, this black faille will go great with that hair of yours and against your skin. Say, God musta put a little blueing in the clay when he made you."

"How's this? Nun's veiling. Say, wouldn't

it be swell in a kind of grey-green to match your eyes?''

But suddenly Orchid, with the bits of fabric in her hand and the girls about her in their cheap imitation dresses of the prevailing modes, was no longer filled with desire. She wanted, instead, soft stuffs of her own selection. Pliable stuffs that could be picked up in bargain-bins and at employés' discount at the Titanic, and that she herself could drape and wind and manipulate about her figure in ways her fingers itched to get at. Fastidious stuffs that her flesh craved. Not stiff serges, but, for the same price, fabrics she had seen in the bargain basement. Stuffs that, when you ran a hand over them, seemed to have to cling a little, of the curious live magnetic quality of silk.

Thus it was that Orchid first came to discover that she could make her own clothes. Frocks out of remnants and next-to-nothings, that were to delight and enhance her.

At seventeen, because of this quality in her of a love and a taste for the batiste and silky things that made her linger in her spare moments around the departments in the store that dealt in them, Orchid, on twelve dollars a week, was in the lingerie department of the Titanic.

All day long the sheer garments rilled

through her fingers. When she ran her hand underneath a bit of silk and spread her fingers under it to point up the webbiness of the pattern or the sheen, she loved the sleazy stuffs. Loved to feel them near the dainty fabric of her own flesh. Dealt in them successfully because she loved the things she sold across the counter.

It was about then that Orchid and a girl in the lace-and-veiling department, named Idaleen Crow, took a room which they shared together in a house on Seventh Avenue below Twenty-third Street. It was a third-storey back, none too large, but with two separate cots, and a closet with a window and a stationary washstand in it that was large enough to use as a sort of dressing-room. They shared it for five dollars a week each. After the years of the institutional life of settlement house and the Clara von Hutten, there was something akin to home in this third-storey back.

Idaleen was rather an odd-looking girl with light blue eyes and brilliant red hair which she wore short as a boy's, long before the craze for docked heads swept the women of half a hemisphere.

Idaleen, who had come from Schenectady for a stage career, complained constantly of the high stuffiness and of the odours of cooking that came across chimney-pots from the world of light housekeepers surrounding them, and of the heat of the sun on the tin roofing opposite.

Orchid complained too. Defensively. She had no way of telling Idaleen that this third-floor back, which you reached by stumbling through a dark hall that was a narrow channel of trash-baskets, approached luxury to her.

A room that was half her own. A room that was not a slit in a tenement or a single cell in a house that smelled of philanthropy. Even the odour of the cans of refuse outside the light housekeepers' doors was preferable to the low embalmed smell of philanthropy.

A room that you could, on a table with a mirror over it that served as dresser, lay out in strips of cotton chintz and a baby pillow on the cot, with a lingerie slip over pink sateen.

The kind of baby pillow that women tucked behind their heads in the motion-pictures.

When Orchid was seventeen and earning twelve dollars a week in the lingerie department and sharing the third-floor back in Seventh Avenue with Idaleen, life already had a shimmer to it.

It was hard sometimes, tucking that one rather lumpy little lingerie pillow behind her neck as she snuggled up for sleep, to realize the years of nights, black vermin-infested nights, that had been childhood to her down in Prince Street.

The Prince Street which no prince ever invaded, and where the little girls, when they played princesses, were princesses the colour of the asphalt jungle.

*

Not that the princes who invaded Seventh Avenue were at all to Orchid's liking.

Or indeed, even to her toleration.

She was frankly scornful of the pimply-jawed, pasty-looking young clerks with no faces in particular, indoor complexions and pinch-back coats with whom Idaleen sat on park benches and in motion-picture theatres and across tall stools at soda-water fountains.

"Life's a compromise. With girls like us it's not what you want, it's what you get," was the philosophy of Idaleen, who had already made her compromise from the dreams of stage triumphs to the reality of the veiling department in the Titanic.

Maybe so. Only Orchid believed passionately in the ultimate attainment of what you want, if somehow, in some way, you could generate within yourself the capacity to want so persistently and so tormentingly that nothing short of achievement could lay the torment.

The things that Orchid wanted! Those

years when the heterogeneity of life in the Titanic beat up about her in a furious kind of tide that blinded the eyes and made the brain flounder, it was not easy to define what she wanted. Even to herself. The vague beauties that she sensed — the dull pain at their remoteness.

Evenings, in the reading-room at the House and later at the Clara von Hutten, that dull pain used to leap at her, even when she did not completely understand it. The look of a poem on the wide white area of a page. Bottled-up beauty in phials of books that somehow withheld their perfume from her. Remoteness of the something. The splendour falls on castle walls. What splendour? She walked down marble halls of the Public Library. Glacial beauty of them. Her own were lined with slops. Somewhere in her reading there had been a poem of girdles and garlands. The girdles and garlands. Her brow was clear for them, and her waist supple. The girdles and the garlands, the friezes above the prosceniums of the motion-picture theatres were gay with them. The girdles and the garlands. . . .

Remoteness of beauty. It was not so much a desire for things in the concrete as it was an ache for the something, she knew not what. Somewhere — beyond — strange beauty of the words that a Settlement House teacher in horn spectacles had once read aloud from Prometheus Unbound. Somewhere beyond — the clasp of girdles and garlands. Her own waist-line so supple, and craving for them.

Somewhere beyond the vista of ninety-eight-cent camisoles and chimney-pots and the smell of slops in the hallway and Idaleen's tawdry patter of "he says" and "she says" and "I says" were beauties that at this time Orchid only sensed with the busy little antennæ of her intuition.

The intuition that presided over the choice of her adjectives and her blouses.

The intuition that led her to pass by the more obvious adornments of Idaleen and the girls of her day-by-day contacts for the inexplicable little refinements which she could not define but which were hers as naturally as the texture of her skin.

The texture of her skin might have helped to explain it. The fine grain of her.

It was easy to continue to wear her straight wing-like hair off her face in a fashion that kept intact its dark-pearl kind of lustre, because the vogue for ornate, artificially waved, rhine-stone-studded coiffures worn by the girls in the store went against that grain.

Orchid could no more have worn one of the

cotton-stitched, cheaply imitative reproductions of Fifth Avenue and Paris models that sold up in the ready-to-wear department as cheaply as nineteen dollars and fifty cents.

Literally, they would have rubbed against her grain.

Evenings, what with the shallow course in designing at the Clara von Hutten to her assistance, Orchid made her own dresses, usually at less than half of the nineteen-fifty. Soft fabrics, that she had picked up in bargain-bins, lying in a swirl about her feet. Sometimes, because her soles were full of sting from the long hours of standing, she propped them, as she sewed, on an opposite chair against an ice-bag, for the blessed coolness.

The girls in the store doubted and debated the authenticity of her esoteric kind of beauty.

"No colour."

"Too frigid."

"Must have been raised on Eskimo Pie."

"That simplicity stuff don't get you anywheres."

"Interesting pallor nothing! I call it jaundice. A box of henna powder would do the same trick for any one of us."

"Wish you had hands like her, do you? Well, better speak to God about that."

There was less controversial discussion of the

quality of Orchid's beauty among the men in the Titanic. To them it was a little glacially dazzling, but there it was!

Some of them asked her to go out with them.

Sometimes she went, of ennui of the evenings in the third-floor rear room and the patter of Idaleen. But more often not.

Dinners in cheap Italian restaurants, where the waiter served heavy soups with a thumb in it, repelled her. Red-ink wines. Jammed subways at theatre-time. Balcony seats. The round stools in front of soda-water stands. Going-home subway jams when a tired neighbour's head was as apt as not to loll over on her shoulder.

And the dreary routine of holding these men who bought her an evening's questionable diversion at the only distance that made them endurable.

There had developed in Orchid, in the years of her harsh schooling in the only world of men she knew, a brittle kind of bitterness.

It was a game to beat them at their own game.

There was something a little exultant about slamming the front door of her rooming-house in the face of a man ramming the toe of his shoe in between, in his effort to follow her upstairs after a theatre, as if by right of the table d'hôte or chop-suey dinner.

There was usually insolence behind the black lashes that veiled Orchid's maltese-grey eyes after the frustration of one of these who had reckoned without his hostess.

Idaleen was one of the girls whose promiscuousness Orchid always had that sense of justifying. And Cora May, also in the veilings and a chum of Idaleen's, who lived "at home."

When Orchid repulsed an impertinence as odious as it was inevitable, it was as if her cruel kind of insolence to the man in question were in the name of the Idaleens and the Cora Mays.

Idaleen and Cora May would have been the first to laugh. Miss Don Quixote out after windmills, if they had known how to put it into words. But just the same it kept Orchid a little less bitter, repudiating in the name of all the girls who did not dare, or did not care, to be selective.

*

One day a girl by the synthetic name of Leland Deland broke her ankle. It occurred in the French room of the Titanic on the first day of a heavily advertised fashion display of imported evening gowns.

She had been walking, in the doll-like fash-

ion of the mannequin, down a short flight of
three coral-carpeted steps; and casually, so that
she scarcely seemed to more than stumble,
twist went her foot in its little jewelled sandal,
so that two bones in the ankle snapped.

To Orchid at that moment selling a ninety-
eight-cent camisole downstairs in the lingerie
department, that mishap was momentous.

There was a jam of women peering over
shoulders in the French room to view this
much-advertised display of a new season's just-
arrived importations. Mostly, it is true,
women who would ultimately go downstairs
and buy a dollar-ninety-eight-cent bungalow-
apron off an aisle sale-table.

Leland Deland was the only girl in the none
too pretentious French department of the great
popular-price store who could lay claim to the
actual qualifications of the professional model.
The other two, both recruited from the Coats
and Dresses, when they walked down the pink
velvet steps had either to pin over the waist-
line or to leave open a hook and eye which
could not make the span.

After the episode of the twisted ankle there
was some quick and futile telephoning.

One of the floormen, who had noticed her
every day as he passed her department on his
way to lunch, suggested Orchid. "There's a

beauty of a pale grey-eyed girl down in the lingerie. Jet-black hair. Effective as the dickens. Might try her."

For the first time in her life, that afternoon Orchid felt the lovely creep of petal-coloured chiffon along her flesh and beheld her whiteness of skin flow down into the sheerness of one French importation after another.

Girdles and garlands. . . .

*

It was curious that the week of the important circumstance of Orchid's permanent promotion from the lingerie to the dual capacity of saleswoman and mannequin in the French room should also have been the week of her first meeting with Martin Innesbrook.

Curious in the way that momentous circumstances often come. In schools. Like porpoises.

The wife of a conspicuous member of the Legislature in Washington had just issued the challenging statement that it was possible for any American woman to be well dressed on three hundred and fifty dollars a year.

In the welter of argument such an expression from a woman prominent in social and diplomatic circles was sure to arouse, Martin Innesbrook was running down a symposium of comment from the angle of the manufacturer of women's wear, the importer, and the consumer.

One of those Sunday feature articles of two-colour illustrations and one-inch title-writing, beloved of American-journalism-for-the-people.

When Orchid, with all the nervousness but certainly none of the gaucherie of the novice, walked down the three coral-coloured steps in a cream-coloured chiffon gown exactly the colour of her own creaminess and with the lustre of her black hair enhanced so that it looked that italicized kind of black that has a blue sheen over it, Martin Innesbrook, who had been standing in a corner of the French room interviewing the head buyer, experienced the sensation of shooting down too quickly in an elevator.

His was typical of the reaction that was making the first appearance of Orchid in the rôle of mannequin a success. His was one of the Oh-ah's that went up as Orchid, with the intuition to properly point her toe and poise before a descent, came down those three rosy steps.

"I think," he said, "I'll get the point of view of the mannequin next. What does the girl who wears the clothes without ever owning them think about it all? That stunning

one over there, with the Egyptian-looking
head and the white skin. I wonder if I could
have a word with her?"

That was how Orchid and Martin Innesbrook met.

It was the first time she had ever known a
man without a "girlie," a "gotta date," a
"kiddo," or a "cutie" in his vocabulary. It
was the first time she had ever encountered a
man who did not regard her with that in-
tangible piggy focus of gaze coming into his
eyes.

It was the first time, standing there after the
fashion show, in a green organdie frock that
felt like surf to her body, and answering with
shy stiff lips the interviewer's terse bombard-
ment of questions, that the remote thing called
beauty had come close enough for her to touch.

*

There was, however, nothing passionately
headlong in the coming-together of these two.
On the contrary, there was a something timid,
and almost, it might have seemed, a something
inhibited about it.

It was a full two weeks after the picture of
her, shy there before him in the green organdie,
had printed itself into his consciousness, before
young Innesbrook, who wanted to seem casual

about it, allowed himself to drop in again at the Titanic.

It was a full two weeks more before Orchid, what with the excitement of the raise in plans and hopes and wages, was able to isolate the one teasing impression that could sometimes seem to make her want to cry: the impression of young Innesbrook, with his straight eyes through horn-rimmed glasses and his dark, damp, excited-looking hair with the furrows of five fingers through it.

It was another two weeks, after a series of desultory, seemingly casual meetings between them, before young Innesbrook could muster up sufficient courage to ask her out to dinner with him in a little restaurant called the Antique which he frequented. A nook of a place above a curio-shop in West Twenty-seventh Street, a few doors from his hotel.

It was the first restaurant of the kind Orchid had ever seen.

Imitation Lowestoft china. Linen doilies in three sizes instead of washable tops or the stained table-cloths of the Italian table d'hôtes. Old prints on the walls and pewter on the plate-racks. Candlelight. Little tucked-away tables for two. It gave her a sense of quiet people at tea-time, over cups that did not rattle, of firelight flickering along old books. A

sense of the niceties. Poor Orchid, feeling out
with the antennæ of her intuition. . . .

*

Vaguely, even before she met Martin, the
name Innesbrook had already worn a place into
her consciousness.

Fact was, every morning on her way to the
Titanic nine out of every ten in the street-car
crush around her, and usually Orchid herself,
were reading *The Enquirer*, an Innesbrook morning paper. *The Daily*, also an Innesbrook illus-
trated sheet, went off the stands like hot cakes.
There was a twenty-eight-storey Innesbrook
office building near Columbus Circle. Innesbrook. Innesbrook. "Are you related to —
what's his name? Max Innesbrook — *the* Max
Innesbrook?"

Martin admitted it rather ruefully.

"Yes, he's my uncle. All the good it has
ever done me! Being related to him is the principal reason I have worked on every daily in
town except one of the Innesbrook chain. In-
considerate, wasn't it, of my father to get himself born a brother to Max? What would seem
to be, offhand, my greatest asset, up to this day
of our Lord hasn't proved to be much except a
liability. If my Uncle Max had fourteen jobs
to hand out and I happened to come along

first, he'd begin with thirteen and count backward."

That was almost the first long speech in the
four weeks of overtures that Martin had made
to Orchid. He delivered it that first evening of
their dinner together in the tea-room up over
the curio-shop.

*

No, there was nothing impetuous about the
beginning of the relationship between these
two. To Orchid it was as if all the uncertain-
ties and the yearnings had been so many little
disks, ringing. And with the coming of Martin they had spun themselves down, into quiet.
Almost into peace.

Here was someone who talked in a low humorous voice. Here was someone removed
from the execrable world of young men in
pinch-back coats; the pasty-faced world of
young men who chewed breath-sweeteners and
felt with their knees against hers under the
tables of the second-rate restaurants.

Here was someone who matched the grain of
her grain.

For the first time in her life a sweet kind of
content was over Orchid.

Once and twice a week, later even three and
four times, in the restaurant above the curio-
shop, after the days in and out of the fine rai-

ment; days that made her feet sting, but most of them days that led to the dinner-hour with Martin. And then, if the weather was fine, walks in the park under star-spangled skies; or sometimes, when a pair of seats came his way from the dramatic department of his newspaper, theatre in orchestra seats, to the smell of furs and of powder on the bare shoulders of women.

It was not that Orchid ever seemed to have anything of real moment to say to Martin. His very cleverness, most of the time, smote her and made her a self-constituted sounding-board for him.

Quick eager things he had to say. Quick as the eager unsaid things she had all her life felt pressing up against her. Martin telling her of his yearnings was like listening to someone full of her own sweet and bitter sickness.

Desire. Ambition. Ways. Means. Fulfillment.

In those early years of what was destined to be his pre-eminence in the field he had chosen, literally she was his sounding-board. A good listener. The recipient of the haphazard contents of a virile mind in quick action.

"Thinking aloud" was what Martin called his mental peregrinations before the silent Orchid. "My thoughts shape up like a grand army while I'm talking to you, Orchid. Things come to me out of thin air. It's because I know you'll trip me up if the ideas don't come clear or if they come shoddy. Never let me get by with intellectual shoddiness, Orchid, or with hokum. You're the best little listener."

Well, she was greedy for the contact with Martin's young mind. It kept her alert.

Sometimes, listening to him, she was ashamed that so much of what was obviously commonplace to him should come to her in the form of a revelation. She would no more have let him know that he was revealing, because there was something pitiable about not having known them all along.

Here were some of the terms he mentioned so casually that he was scarcely conscious of them, but that sent Orchid scurrying to the en-cyclopædia in the book-department of the Ti-tanic, or to the library reference-room those evenings she did not dine with him:

Mount Shasta. Germ-plasm. Inferiority complex. Social revolution. Pistachio nuts. Darwinian Theory. Succinct. Sinn Fein. Law of Gravitation. Thomas Hardy. Stravinsky. Anatomy of Melancholy. Hedda Gabler. Lenin. Anatole France. Manchester Guardian. Arabia Deserta. Michelangelo. Ipso facto. Artichokes. Australasia. Pedicure. Louvre.

Robert Browning. Elizabeth Browning. Robert Frost. Psychology. Ethical Culture. Free verse. Renaissance. Crusader. Cloisonné. Ionic. Epictetus. Daniel Boone. Helen of Troy. Protoplasm. Sauté. Decline and Fall of the Roman Empire. Cabal. Hague. Holy See. Vesta Tilly. Laocoön. Electron. Beowulf. Chaise longue. Confucius. Anthropology. Havelock Ellis. Lapis Lazuli. Martinique. Tagore. Bacardi. Paderewski. Seine. Monograph. Scotti.

Small wonder she was a good listener. Martin in his most casual moods was an intellectual panorama.

"Hang it, if I get myself elected president of the Bromide Club for saying it, I'll repeat it again and again: you're wonderful, Orchid. You *do* understand."

"Why shouldn't I, Martin? The things you want so passionately for yourself are just my way of wanting other things for myself."

"Yes, only I don't give you much chance to dwell upon them. Sometimes, though, Orchid, I want to hear them all. Your life has been so extraordinary. So like a book." And then, man-like, because hers was a listening eager face, off he was again on the subjects of the desires that crowded his young horizon.

"You know, Orchid, there's a certain advantage, after all, in having my uncle so pig-headed about giving me a chance on one of his papers. It gets a fellow's fighting blood up."

"Of course, Martin. That's what I've been trying to tell you right along. He's getting you on your mettle in order to make sure that you have it."

"Oh, he'd give me a job all right, I guess, if I'd do him the good to come right out and ask for it. I tell you, Orchid, a self-made man with thirty millions, nineteen newspapers, unlimited political power, and the authority to surround himself with a Yes-Yes Club fifty-two weeks of the year, is bound to get mental astigmatism. A man along toward the apex of his achievements needs specs. Some day those specs will be me."

Oh yes. Oh yes. The two young wiseacres of them nodding their heads above the candles on the table between them.

"Stands to reason a man cannot have grown into a Crœsus and a sort of imitation Julius Cæsar without getting a little bone-headed with authority.

Crœsus. Julius Cæsar. Orchid at taking her mental notes.

"My father used to say of him, up to the very day he died: 'Your Uncle Max has only one yardstick for measuring humanity. And that is the yardstick of himself, which is thirty-seven inches long.'"

"Martin, no wonder you're clever, to have had a father who could say that!"

"And yet my father was never anything more to my uncle than a half-maudlin poet of a college professor. He was too fine-grained for my uncle to understand."

"Like you, Martin."

"Lord, no. I'm a rhinoceros as to hide and heart. I won't be squelched. Kick me out of one door, I bob in the next. I want that editorial job on an Innesbrook sheet. Hang it, I do. For reasons. For very private reasons of my own. Can't you guess, Orchid?"

"Martin — how can I?"

And then Martin flushing up and running away from the subject as if for fear it might pursue him.

"It's his stubbornness as much as anything that riles me. The stubbornness of the old man saying I have to earn my right to work on an Innesbrook paper. Why, I've written feature articles that have attracted enough attention to have editors competing a little for my services. There are dozens of fellows working on his papers throughout the country who haven't earned the right as much as I have, whatever that means."

"Just the same, Martin, and don't you forget it, your Uncle Max sees your feature pages in the *Express* every Sunday."

"Well, if he does he keeps pretty darn mum about it, and I'll certainly never be the one to call his attention to them. I know my aunt and the girls call his attention to them, but for all the old man ever says, lots of good it does me. Know what? I think I'm an idiot to go out there week-ends. I'd rather stay in town and just loaf it out with you, Orchid."

"But, Martin, it is important that you keep up the connection."

"What is the sense of being a guest at Innesbrook-on-the-Hudson, if I cannot even meet my uncle on a man-to-man basis? Sunken gardens, Italian rococo, country-estate stuff doesn't even mean the dollar and fourteen cents' worth of my railroad ticket to me. I'm tired of having to beard the old gentleman in his gymnasium every time I want a few minutes' real talk with him."

"But, Martin, a man who has accomplished what he has, it should be sort of a liberal education just to be around him. After all, he *is* Max Innesbrook, you know."

"That's it. Hang it, Orchid, I want so passionately what I want. And he has accomplished what I want. But not the way I want

[133]

to accomplish. His success means just wealth and power to him. He's lost sight, in the dust of the struggle, of the ideal behind the fight."

"Dear, dear Martin, don't you!"

"Journalism to him is just a brilliant means to a brilliant end. Power. Money. Position. But I want success in journalism because I know it to be the most potent force for good and public service in our civilization. I don't believe a civilization moulds its journalism. I think journalism can do much to determine the calibre of the civilization it interprets."

Eager young Martin with his flaming case thrust there above the candle-flame.

"Yes, Martin, yes." Sweet receptive acquiescence of Orchid, which set his ardent young ego to glowing.

"I want to own a chain of newspapers some day that will instruct, not mollify. Defy the wrong, not compromise with it or aid or abet it. I want to educate readers instead of cram them with the kind of stuff they squall for. It's like feeding bananas to babies, much of the journalism of to-day. Give them what they want whether it's good for them or not. The point is, it pays. I tell you, Orchid, the press is the greatest instrument for good or evil in the history of the world. It's the flaming sword of civilization."

MANNEQUIN

"And you are going to carry it, Martin. See if you don't."

"Orchid, when you talk like that, I — I feel I could move empires! I tell you, some day, even with the handicap of being a great man's nephew, journalism is going to know I'm here!"

"Indeed it is, Martin. You're more than just an aspirant. You're a — a — crusader!"

"You darling!"

It was the first time, on that explosive of Martin's, that there fell between the two an instant of frightened and awkward and ecstatic silence.

*

Orchid was being noised about in the trade. An importer from West Thirty-fourth Street had sent one of his foreladies over to the French room of the Titanic, ostensibly to browse about as a shopper, but actually on the private mission of getting a glimpse of the Egyptian-looking girl said to wear clothes with unusual effect.

Three days later, two offers came to Orchid almost simultaneously. The first, from an importer in West Thirty-seventh Street, was for her services as mannequin at a salary of eighteen dollars a week.

And that very same day, to climax that considerable climax, probably the most exclusive firm of dressmakers on two continents, Drecotte Fils of Rue de la Paix, Nice, Palm Beach, Newport, Fifth Avenue, made her an offer to come to the New York branch to show clothes at twenty-two dollars a week.

When Orchid found a telephone at lunchhour to tell Martin about it, her voice, from being breathless, went over the wire to him in little clumps.

*

First of all, it meant the end of the thirdfloor back, all jammed up there with the tawdriness of Idaleen. The whole of two Sundays Orchid trudged on one of the most delightful missions she had ever known. House-hunting, for a room of her very own that she intended to share with no one. For a room to which she could now afford to give the little touches her fastidiousness craved.

Irrelevantly enough, when Orchid visualized this room of her heart's desire, more than any one prized possession, she saw one object. An object which to her symbolized the new era of niceties into which she was about to enter.

Orchid wanted a room with the sill-space for a window-box! A green-painted one in which she could plant growing things. It epitomized for her, without her realizing it, all her suppressed desires for the garden places. The smell of sweet things. The growing of green things.

She found such a room. In East Seventeenth Street. A street of former brown-stone grandeur, going down none too debonairly before the elbowing-in of the rooming-houses.

For twelve dollars a week, more than she had a right to afford, Orchid, after lodging-house after lodging-house that smelled of cold boiled potato and roach-powder, capitulated to the first-floor, ex-grand-salon parlour of the house in Seventeenth Street.

Offhand there was not much to commend the room except, after the rounds of the lodging-houses, the dignity of its size, and the two long windows that looked out over the sidewalk and opened on to iron-work balconies, too small for any purpose save window-boxes! The wrought-iron little curvatures of balcony on a level with the top of the stoop helped.

It was the kind of room, in fact, that could strike the despair of a damp dreary day to your soul.

The solemn, ornate pier-glass, ceiling-high between two lank windows. The erstwhile gleaming crystal chandelier that was bare now of its gleaming prisms and lean as a picked old bone. The brown marble fireplace with the

look to it of mausoleum, and the tunnel-
shaped grate.

A dreary moor of a room; and yet to Orchid,
who had tramped and tramped and seen how
drearier than a moor most of the lodgings could
be, this lean brown parlour, set out in curlicue
plush pieces of the McKinley period and the
combination odds and ends of what had once
been a "parlour set," mixed in with such practical addenda as couch and wash-stand, suggested possibilities.

First, the window-boxes. Fresh flowers in an
imitation majolica vase from the Titanic basement, on that little marble shelf across the base
of the pier-glass, would help.

And cretonnes. Orchid, by way of the little
strips of it on the dresser of her third-floor
back, had learned the secret of the proper use
of these gay stuffs. A few yards of leaf-and-bud
design would cover the outlines of curlicue imitation mahogany and mangy old plush and
light up the old room out of its musty swoon.

For the first time in her life, when she paid
the landlady a deposit of five dollars that grey
Sunday afternoon, Orchid had a corner she
could literally call her own.

On her way back to her room she routed
out a carpenter on Third Avenue, by ringing a
bell marked "Night and Holidays," and gave

him the order for the window-boxes. Green ones with little swelling fronts to match the shape of the two iron balconies.

*

The first time Martin came to see her in the new quarters, he stood in the doorway and let out a whistle. A long, slow, low, surprised whistle. Mostly to cover up a curious emotion that rose to his throat at her having achieved it all on the rather pitiful oddments and endments within her reach.

It was a pleasant room of cretonne, glow of geranium, bits of brass, and a tea-cart that caught the firelight. The tea-table had come from a second-hand shop on Third Avenue. Only two dollars and seventy-five cents, because the plate-glass top was cracked. The cretonnes, too, not that you would have guessed it, came from a bargain-basement, and the frames of the subdued prints of the Coliseum, Watts's Hope, and Michelangelo's Hand of God were just passe-partout that had been dulled with sandpaper.

There was a Windsor chair in the little ell beside the mantelpiece, bought in the natural pine in a kitchen-supply department of the Titanic and stained the Italian walnut colouring of the tea-table. The screen around the baby electric stove and refrigerator was of green grass cloth in a yellow oak frame, but surprisingly redeemed with quaint old pictures, reminiscent of Godey's Lady's Book, which had been cut out and pasted against the grass cloth.

The horrific lace curtains with the design of drape woven into them had been replaced by cretonne with a coloured bead fringe. A wicker chair with a foot-rest that drew out and a little rack on the side for magazines and books was drawn in beneath a lamp made from a slightly damaged cloisonné vase, with a shade of cretonne edged in the coloured beads.

To Martin, who had repeatedly heard about the slit of room in Prince Street that represented Orchid's ancestral manor, and the lore of the barge-father and the early environment of the child whose parent, between spurts of affection, could be so strangely alien, there was something about this brave show of room that caught him by the throat.

"Good Lord. Poor little one. Out of nothing, too."

"You like it, Martin?"

"Like it! Why, it's as dainty as you are."

"I did it all — with my little hatchet."

"With your little spunk, you mean. It's a corking room. It's a grand room. It's a room of a room, all right. Don't see how you ever managed to achieve it out of somebody's old rag-tag of a horror of a salon-parlour."

"After a week-end at your uncle's lovely place, it must seem like a slum to you."

"Like heaven to me."

"Oh, Martin, I've an electric stove here behind this screen, and the duckiest aluminum griddle for chops. And lettuce! A whole wet towel of it in my brand little, new little refrigerator, and the heavenliest strawberries, *yum-yum!* Do let's stay and fix dinner here. It will help our economy and our digestion."

That was the beginning of three and sometimes four a week of these delicious meals of home concoction. Usually, afterward, with the last dish dried between them, Martin read aloud, Orchid with the creeping sweetness of domestic serenity out over her as she sat on a stool in the circle of light from the cretonne-shaded lamp.

Or Martin, who loved to compose aloud, dictated part of his next week's feature article to Orchid until her fingers were numb from their crouching haste to get it down in longhand.

"Orchid, I've an idea for an article on prison reform! All this talk about the segregation of criminals, cell hygiene, capital punishment, is putting the cart before the horse. Now my idea is this!"

Or: "How's this for an idea, Orchid? I was reading somewhere the other day that the estimated intelligence of the average motion-picture audience in this country is said to be that of an eleven-year-old child. That practically means that the intellectual target to shoot at in this country is that of a backward adult. What's to be done to get at the root of it? Jove, if I write that one, I'm going to see to it that Aunt Em slips a copy of it under my uncle's breakfast napkin for fifteen consecutive mornings."

Or: "His daily paper is the workingman's university. You see, I've the popular angle, Orchid. I'm a congenital low-brow. I think in terms of the lingo of the people. Now if ever I own a newspaper of my own ——"

"You will, Martin. Many of them. You will."

"I will if the right kind of incentive has anything to do with it. Orchid, if I stop to think about, you know what? Well, it's this: If these Sunday feature articles of mine are amounting to anything at all, I've you to thank for it. You've been such a brick with your sympathy and receptive kind of mind. Just inspiration, that's what you are!"

"Nonsense, Martin. You've been a liberal education for me."

"How's this for an idea? Now, take the public-playground situation in this town. There ought to be some way to educate the people to realize that until they become more acutely self-conscious of the needs of their children, our slums are going to continue to breed undersized human beings. The parents themselves are the ones who must clamour for more park-room and more sun-room and not depend upon the efforts of a few philanthropic societies. Now my idea is this ———"

"Now my idea is this." It must be admitted that, in those days of his mind in the making, he would hurl out with the vehemence of a thunderbolt a premise that could sometimes go off like a damp firecracker. But then there were more to hurl. And more. But, all in all, there were enough good sound explosives in each packet to make him arresting, even in those early years.

Sometimes, it is true, Orchid did contribute to those ideas. Indeed, once brilliantly, suggesting a reform in the vocational training in the public schools that not only helped accomplish the ultimate adoption of her plan, but brought in Martin an order for three subsequent articles on the same topic.

"Now my idea is this." Dear Martin. Often in those early days before their complete realization that this thing was love between them swept over her, Orchid kept thinking herself a little maternal toward him.

*

Every day at Drecotte's, even though arms and legs sometimes felt completely numb from the fatigue of long fittings or paradings through the show-room, was full of a very certain kind of delight.

The delight of box after box coming in from the Customs House to be unwrapped of its smother of tissue-paper wrappings. Gowns to be lifted out. Brocades. Sheaths of satin. Organdies fraily stiff enough to stand alone. Embroideries. Parasols. Hats. Nonsense feather fans in brilliant tropical plumage. Sachet. Handkerchiefs made of web. Nightgowns of pleated chiffon with thread-lace yokes the shape of butterflies.

And at Drecotte's the gowns had names! Softy nonsenses. Minette. Seraph. Brown Betty. Jonquil. Ambre. Nazimova. Godiva. Opaline. To Orchid they had the lustre of petals.

All day long when she was not "showing" in the mauve and mirrored costume-room, it was a matter of standing, along with others of the girls, in the bare fitting-room to the constant whir of sewing-machines, in gowns that were being built along the model lines of her figure.

Occasionally there were free half-hours when the girls huddled in the badly aired dressing-rooms, in the muslin wrappers they wore over their silk knickerbockers, for talk and hot coffee. But usually Orchid preferred even the limb-splitting fatigue of the fittings to these social periods with the mannequins.

There were six of them at Drecotte's. Toto, a flaring red-and-black girl with a Spanish accent, but said to have been born Rosenbaum in Brooklyn. There was Denise, a transparently fair figurine of a blonde; the pellucid kind of fairness, as if the shadow of worldliness had never crossed the Mediterranean blue of her eyes, though she had once figured notoriously in an unsuccessful breach-of-promise suit with the son of a copper magnate. Cyd, who wore tailored clothes better than any girl in her profession, and who had a yellow third finger from too constant smoking. Myrrh, an almost grotesquely slender girl with a head shaped like an egg and yellow hair which she wore parted in the middle and slicked down as if it were painted on. Clarice, with a flare of orange-coloured curly hair that made her look like a chrysanthemum, and the loveliest white skin and young moon of a silhouette. When Clarice opened her full red lips you were dumbfounded and abashed by the torrent of poison that could issue from them.

Sometimes the plain clapboard dressing-room where these girls held their confabs could seem to Orchid to crowd up as if with myriads of pestilent insects. Talk. Talk. Talk. The grim, the wise, the disillusioned patter of incredibly grim, wise, disillusioned girls.

Clarice, who was met every evening at closing by a turfman of international reputation, and who wore a diamond-and-emerald anklet underneath her ten-dollar silk stockings, had shed her illusions as easily as she shed the white muslin wrappers. She usually sat about the dressing-room in only the pink underthings that matched the colour and texture of her flesh.

"What don't getcha anywhere isn't worth getting. If I hear a fellow is on the level, I know it's the lower level. If the guy offers you lobster, it don't mean he's showing you a good time. It means he's beating you to it before you see terrapin lower down on the bill of fare. Never fall for a fellow who offers you his diamond stud in the presence of a third party. He'll take it back later. Me for the fellow who gives you a string of pearls in a vinegar cruet.

A fellow did that to me once. 'What's the big idea?' I said to him when I unwraps a vinegar cruet. 'For the luvva, what's the big idea?' Then I see. Real pearls. Vinegar can't touch them!''

These were some of the fragrant brand of aphorisms from the lips of Clarice, matched in no very different key by Toto, Denise, Myrrh, and Cyd.

It meant that, after the first month of sitting on the edge of it in a tight hard ball of repugnance, it was borne poignantly and frighteningly home to Orchid that the smouldering resentment of her colleagues was breaking out at her in little spirts of flame.

"There's no girl ever worked in this firm had the chance to turn down going on a party twice,'' said Toto one noon hour, when the models were having sandwiches and pie-à-la-mode brought in, narrowing her eyes and blowing cigarette smoke unmistakably in the direction of Orchid, seated in her white muslin wrapper on the edge of the fitting-dais and munching her sandwich.

"Toto, I would have come, but I — I already had my evening taken.''

"Like hell you did. I never would have asked you to come out on it, far as I was concerned. It was my boy friend had a friend who saw you at the Ambassador fashion-show in a lacquer red. Must have been Duval's Mimi. 'Is your friend an ice-man?' I says to my friend, when he asks me to bring you along on a party. 'Whatta you mean, "ice-man"?' he says. 'Well,' I says to him, I says, 'it will take one to move her, because she's a cake of ice herself.'"

"Toto, you know that's not true."

"Well, if it isn't," quoth Toto in the husky tones peculiar to her, "come over to my place to-night and bring your boy friend. What do you know, girls? Little melt-in-your-mouth brings down an Innesbrook off the branch. Straight shot, I'll say. Oh, I've got the dope all right. Horn-rimmed high-brow starting low down with a reporter's job. The boy wonder. Bring him along. Can't promise you anything soaking wet, but we can be properly damp upon occasion, can't we, girls?"

Poor Orchid, she was literally afraid of the wall of ostracism these grim-eyed, wise-eyed, doll-faced ones were ready to erect about her. The wall that would surely, subtly, inevitably make unendurable the days among them and crowd her out of Drecotte's.

"Toto, I can't to-night. I've a previous en——"

"Didn't I tell you!"

"No. No. Girls, please! I want to come, but I can't to-night. I have it! Now, why won't you girls, all four of you, come down to my place sometime?"

"Sometime? Sure. How's July thirty-fourth? Nineteen ninety-nine."

"No. No. I mean, how's Saturday night? I never have engagements over the week-ends. I — all of you, come down to my place."

"Oh, a knitting bee?"

"No. No. Bring your friends, your — your boy — friends."

"Sure, we'll come," said Toto, and stared at her with the look of a small boy impaling a butterfly. "Sure, we'll come. Gladta. Won't we, girls? Muchabliged."

"Sure, we'll come."

*

Well, there was no use worrying about it. It was one of those things one simply had to go through with. It could not be so bad as one dreaded. Besides, Martin, on his week-end at Innesbrook, would not be there to witness her in intimate association with these girls.

It was one thing relating to Martin the topics and incidents of her workaday, but somehow it was quite another to have him see her on a close social basis with these girls whose language could hop off their lovely lips like so many toads. She shrank from that.

But inviting them was part of the wise policy of placating them for what they considered her assumption of little superiorities, and for such strokes of fortune as her having been chosen to go to Philadelphia for the fashion-show at the Belvedere, and for the fact that the loveliest of the costumes, tailored ones too, were now falling to the lot of Orchid whenever the most fastidious customers were out in the show-room.

There was, of course, a certain exhilaration that went with it. Try as she would, Orchid could not keep down the little glows of satisfaction. It was worth having to placate the girls. Just as it was worth having to invite Cyd, the day that she was sent to Long Beach in her place to wear sports togs, out to lunch beforehand and buying her Parma violets that cost five dollars a bunch.

*

Orchid was proud of her room.

It was April, and the windows were open and the curtains looped back to show the glow of the flower-boxes. The mantel had been cleared and laid out with a buffet supper of cold cuts and stuffed tomatoes, mounds of chicken salad with mayonnaise and pimento criss-crosses, and cool stalks of celery with cream cheese in the groove.

It would have been easier getting it all from the corner delicatessen, except that fastidiousness revolted from the odour of show-case salads and of mayonnaise weltering in that closeness. And so, taking her cue from the only criterion she knew, delicatessen food-displays, the salad was home-and-Orchid-made, chopped and mixed on a little table behind the Godey screen, and the sandwiches too. Also a dainty fruit salad, built up in layers to a peak surmounted with a tiny American flag.

There was grape-juice punch in a bowl rented from a neighbourhood confectioner's, and coffee in the percolator the girls used in the dressing-room, and a basket of fruits and candies that Martin had sent before he left for Innesbrook.

He had wanted to remain in town that weekend but there were two cardinal reasons why Orchid urged him so to go. The second she was not quite honest about, even with herself. First, her desire that he lose no opportunity to ingratiate himself at Innesbrook. And, secondly, the not-so-frank reason of not wanting him to see her in the only social environment she could boast. The girls, even though you tempered your judgments of them, were not companions to be proud of.

Toto brought her turfman. He was all bulbous when he arrived, and clinked and aroused peals of laughter. The bulbs and clinks were bottles tucked up grotesquely under his coat. There was even one down inside the back of his waistcoat, which Toto extricated by climbing on a chair and diving for it. He was a great chunk of a fellow with a face made familiar to even the slavey who opened the door for him by the frequent newspaper prints of it. And when he threw back his head and laughed, which he did upon slightest occasion, the room, literally, the lamp on the table and the tea-things on the wagon, rattled.

Early in the evening, even though it was mild spring, the fumes and the hilarity mounted so high that Orchid closed the long windows of her first-floor room, that looked out directly on the sidewalk, and drew the cretonne curtains.

Cyd, in grotesque contrast that somehow made one shiver, arrived in one of the mannish-looking outfits so characteristic of her, the inevitable cigarette drooping from her stained third finger, and accompanied by a lily-looking youth of not more than twenty, who bore the name of a family that had been outstanding in American social history for generations. A lily youth who strummed all evening upon a curious moaning instrument he had brought from a recent journey to India, and who drank his highballs through a silver pocket-straw, a method which must have had an effectiveness all its own, so peculiarly it seemed to intoxicate him. Slowly. A little languidly. Amorously, so that his long white hands placed themselves against you whenever you chanced to pass him, like pale, horrid, slightly damp flowers.

Clarice came with a shellacked-haired companion, his arm in a sling from a recent polo accident, who bore the important commercial name of Brangwyn. He brought along the "friend" who had seen Orchid wear the gown called Mimi at the Ambassador fashion-show. Allen Terry. A blond young man with a bit of clipped moustache, very long legs which he crossed twice when he sat down, wrapping himself in himself, and a flat gold cigarette-case, with his monogram in diamonds, protruding from his waistcoat pocket. Long fingers that stepped constantly along a narrow pearl-and-platinum chain across his waistcoat. Cream-coloured spats. The Terry-Paper-Mills Terry.

There was nothing outstanding about him.

He had the usual manner of these men with girls of this group. The flippant easy manner of unreserve. The manner that Orchid had dreaded so for Martin to ever see her subjected to. The manner that had something of an insidious where-do-we-go-from-here suggestion to it. Young men who did not rise from their chairs when one of these girls entered a room. Young men who were always batting about with their hands eager to touch them, pinch at their cheeks; troll hands along their waistlines.

There was nothing to differentiate young Terry, except perhaps the quick noisy effect of the highballs upon him. Almost immediately loud, obstreperous, and eager to achieve the state of being "on a party," he was the principal reason for having to draw the curtains and lower the windows to enclose the fumes.

One hated his touch and the moist lips with a little trickle of saliva at the corners. By the unwritten law of such occasions, however, young Terry was Orchid's pairing-off partner. He kept plaiting and unplaiting a silk tassel that hung from her girdle and driving her with it as if it were a rein. "Giddy-ap! Whoa there, my Beauty." And laughing in an obstreperous fashion which she feared would penetrate beyond the room; and all the while his face so close to hers that she could feel the hot fannings of his breath.

It was a party of two's. There was no breaking up these two's. Clarice had frankly installed herself on Brangwyn's lap early in the evening and would not be pried off. Toto, feeding sandwiches to her turfman, held the morsel for him to nibble and then tilted his flask to his lips for him to wash it down, alternating with an occasional sip herself.

The kind of party that ran meticulously true to form. The kind of party expected of rich young bounders and a group of the town's picked mannequins.

Moving through the course of that long tempestuous evening, the insatiable young Terry more and more at the reins of her sash, sometimes it seemed to Orchid, as the fumes and hilarity mounted, that she must be walking through some sort of delirium. The delirium of horrid too-close lips, the smell of powder on stale flesh, the damp white horrid hands of men, the reek of pocket-flasks, the nauseous twanging moan of that little musical instrument out of India.

She sat trying not to seem tense as the noises kept mounting, but all the time her toes were in clumps in her slippers with the growing fear that this party might leap its bounds.

What if, by unforeseen mischance, Martin were to walk in and find her being driven, to the idiocies of young Terry, from corner to corner of the room by the silver tassel? What if the neighbours were to complain of the revelry? Or Mrs. Snuggs, the mole of a landlady, who usually kept pretty close to her underground apartments? The inflamed face of young Terry drawing in the rein closer and closer. Terrifyingly closer, although with her manner she remained so remote. So amiable in an alien little way she had. And, paradoxically enough, it was just this quality, the fine coat of offishness over her amiability, that seemed to inflame Terry into the noisiness. Her secret loathing of him. Her secret fear of him. Her secret fear of the mounting informality of the group within the sanctity of her very own dear room.

The room of the quiet evenings with Martin.

The room suddenly desecrated.

And surely enough, horridly enough, humiliatingly enough, the party did leap its bounds. The pocket-flasks. The lolling heads of girls. The sprawling young men. The mounting of laughter that was more and more unrestrained.

One knew with dread of heart, even before peering through the drawn curtains, that there would be a group assembled on the sidewalk.

MANNEQUIN

And there it was forming. Of neighbours. Of passers-by. Of loiterers.

Once young Terry clamped Orchid down to his lap; and while she beat at his chest with her fists, fighting him angrily off, but trying with a knot of hysteria in her throat to seem laughing, there, there it came! Oh, oh, oh! The shame of it. Bang, bang. That must be Mrs. Snuggs now, up from her basement bedroom to protest at the nuisance.

The public nuisance taking place in Orchid's room. Her flesh shrank, feeling as if it were running downhill from her body in shivers. Orchid, clamped there in Allen Terry's lap trying to pummel herself clear of the horridness of him, and Mrs. Snuggs walking in.

It was three o'clock of that hilarity-ridden morning, with Orchid jammed there and pummelling young Terry's chest, when Mrs. Snuggs, with her hair in a pug surrounded by curl-papers and a none-too-fastidious wrapper with three absurd ruffles on it over her nightdress, invaded the inflamed occasion of what was to be Orchid's first and last attempt to maintain the grace of good standing with her colleagues.

At a little after three of that morning, it was her humiliation, not unmixed with a certain secret gloating satisfaction, to behold Allen

Terry ejected in the ignominious fashion of being led by the outraged Mrs. Snuggs to the top of the brown-stone steps, shoved, and, if she could have endured to look further, landed at the bottom of them in a sliding position.

For days after the occasion of the ejection of that party forcibly from her room, Orchid went about with two pink mats of sting against her cheeks. Of the ignominy.

The girls laughed about it for weeks. Young Terry in his horizontal slide down the stoop. Toto trying to pull herself together. Myrrh, careening as if she were chasing her cigarette smoke. The irate Mrs. Snuggs in her sight of a blue cotton wrapper with three sateen ruffles at the hem.

There was a sense of new camaraderie in the dressing-room.

Orchid belonged now.

She had never felt so close to Martin as when his hand stole over hers as her voice slipped into tears as she told him about it. The humiliation. The dousing, searing humiliation. Mrs. Snuggs, and the subtle insolence of manner, too, that she had dared to show since the ejection of the party.

Martin knew Terry. The Terry estate was up in the direction of Innesbrook. Sometimes Terry dropped in for a game of tennis with Martin's cousin, Celeste Innesbrook, and occasionally he helped to make up a foursome. Yes, Martin knew Terry. He was the sort that would call a tennis-ball out of bounds when it was three inches in. He had been expelled from Yale. For reasons — well, just for reasons. Dear Martin, with his way of not letting anyone take the disagreeable facts of life seriously.

That was the evening, sitting there in the room that had somehow been desecrated by the party, with Martin trying to divert her from the worrying subject, that something really pleasant happened; and later, out of that same occasion, something not only pleasant, but approaching the first real ecstasy she had ever known.

She had been telling Martin, in a voice jerked with tears, the story of the wretched occasion up to the debasing climax and the entrance of Mrs. Snuggs.

Suddenly Martin, to divert her, caught up the evening paper and began turning its pages.

"Forget it, Orchid. Who won the ball-game? There's no use stewing about a situation over which you had no control. Terry is a rotter. Always has been a rotter. Hurrah for Mathewson, there's the baseball boy of this season! Cheer up, Orchid, and the next time I see old landlady Snuggs I'll tell her that ejection by the scruff of the neck is better than he is used to. Whew! I see where a professor in a small up-state college has been fired because he interpreted Genesis in terms of geological eras instead of seven days. What this country is ready for is another series of controversial Darwin-Bible articles."

Darwin. Orchid always making the secret little notes. Darwin. Genesis.

"Well, what do you know! Listen to this, Orchid. The Scott woman went free. I knew they would never get a male jury to convict her!"

"No!"

"Yep. And that woman murdered her husband as sure as I'm sitting in this chair."

"Of course she did. Why, she all but admitted it!"

"Some day I want to do a series of articles on the jury system as it is and as ——"

"Martin! I have it!"

"What?"

"It!"

"What is it?"

"An idea!"

"My dearest, you excite me strangely."

"But I'm serious, Martin."

"Of course you are, dear. Now what?"

"I know a series of articles that is simply

shrieking to be written. By you. What this country needs is to be aroused to a situation pointed up by this Scott case. That the women of America can literally get away with murder. Witness the Scott case. Take the Madge Ellington case. Everybody is talking about the fact that a woman murderer who indulges in a fit of shooting is acquitted, but nobody is doing anything about it. There is your chance to stir up what you call latent public pyschology. Why, Martin, you could sell that idea even to your uncle."

In the circle of lamplight Martin looked at her slowly, and with little of the gusto with which he sometimes spouted ideas, only to reject them.

"Shouldn't wonder," he said. "This does make at least the fifth acquittal of an obviously guilty woman in the last two years. Shouldn't wonder, Orchid. S'pose I was to write in this vein: Give the woman murderer her chance for punishment! That sounds Innesbrooky enough.

"Precisely. If women want their suffrage, they should be given the whole of it."

"The whole hog. Exactly. Here is all this hullabaloo about the vote, and, now that they have it, never in the history of crime has there been so much discrimination between the sexes.

Why, Lucretia Borgia to-day would have a cinch."

Lucretia Borgia. There was a new one again!

"This country just won't let a woman murderer take her punishment."

"Women should fall as well as stand on their rights, Martin."

"You're saying something!"

"But in the last analysis it's not the women so much, Martin, as the men themselves. The sentimental, false chivalry of the male jury. Why, didn't you read, right in this very Scott case, where the Judge had to resort to having a screen put around Mrs. Scott while she sat in the witness-chair, so the jury couldn't get a peep at her pretty ankles?"

"There's the Innesbrook angle for you!"

"It's a joke and a crying social outrage at the same time, Martin."

"The chance of a lifetime to rouse public sentiment against sentimentality."

"If one after another woman murderer and social offender is to be acquitted, Martin, why, the entire system of social equality for the sexes is a farce, ip-so fac-to!"

Suddenly Martin sprang to his feet.

"I'm going home now and do enough of one to have it under my arm when I arrive at Innesbrook to-morrow. There's a life-size germ in the judge-and-the-screen idea. My uncle is too good a newspaper man not to see it."

"Martin!"

"Orchid," cried Martin, and spun her to him. "I can't wait much longer. If I can only get on my feet, and these articles are as apt to put me there as anything that has ever happened to me, we can marry then. I love you. Orchid. There is no use trying to hold it back any longer. I love you. I want to marry you. I'm pretty rotten as a Romeo, but, Orchid — I — gee, I like you."

"Martin — the things you know about me — things — Nana — everything — Nana — me— after all you know ——"

"After all I know! You mean because of all I know about you. About your sweetness, your dearness, your darling untouchedness. Orchid, I love you."

*

After this, because she had established a sort of proprietorship over this series, Martin was guilty of a not infrequent performance which he would have admitted before no newspaper man living.

It was a lifelong weakeness of his that he liked to think out loud. Talking to Orchid was like cranking the dynamo of his machine. The machine of his brain.

Sometimes the luxury of a telephone, which Orchid allowed herself in order to save the long narrow flight that led to the public slot-machine outside Mrs. Snuggs's sleeping-room, jangled as late as eleven o'clock at night.

Invariably it was Martin, bent either on luring her out to a little coffee-house near Times Square, frequented by journalists, or on trying out on her over the wire a phrase or a page quotation.

Sometimes the call came even later than eleven, awakening her, and from his end Martin would give her time to throw a blanket across her shoulders, get her feet into slippers, and cuddle up with the receiver to her ear while, with his invariable and irrepressible enthusiasm for the just-completed piece of work, he read over the telephone.

"Pretty good stuff?"

"Martin, it's one of your best!"

"You darling! Sure you like the reference to old Judge V. Cleary. Think it's a bit too strong?"

"Indeed, if anything, it's not strong enough."

"Now go back to bed, darling goose, and thanks for being a darling goose."

MANNEQUIN

He loved to call her out of bed into her snug coil at the other end of the wire, to listen and, of course, to applaud.

That was how he telephoned her this night, twice after he had left her. It was thrilling, lifting the cretonne doll before she raised the receiver; thrilling to know that there, it was Martin again!

"Orchid, sweetheart, I can't sleep."

"Neither can I, Martin."

"It's so wonderful having got it said."

"It's so wonderful having heard it said."

"I love you, Orchid."

"I love you, Martin."

"Dear Silly."

"Dear Silly."

"Orchid, I've one article all blocked out and a second ready to take shape. Sort of a series would be bully."

"Martin, not really!"

"Yes; couldn't wait to get at them. Old gentleman doesn't come to town on Fridays. I'll be out at Innesbrook by the time you're reporting for work to-morrow morning. I'll beard him in his gym. I'll make him listen. The stuff just bristles with phrases of yours. How's this one: 'Sexless Justice'? And this: 'Is sex equality merely a phrase to make the male feel more at his ease for keeping his seat

[165]

before the female strap-hanger?' You're my little collaborator, all right. My life-time collaborator, all right!"

"Martin, you're wonderful."

"If I am, you've made me that way. It was all your idea."

"You're wonderful."

"You're wonderful."

"Good-night, my dearest."

"Good-night, my dearest dear."

Long after the receiver was up again and the cretonne telephone-doll replaced, she sat there reluctant to uncoil herself from the attitude that Martin's words, coming over the wire, had made into an attitude of ecstasy.

*

The beauty of Innesbrook was the beauty of dark green shade of oak and poplar, view of Hudson where it widens out like a lake, and a Georgian house that was mostly width. An almost semi-circular house, all the rooms over-looking both the front and back gardens at once, and windows that seemed to be without frames because their stone-work was hidden behind the ivy flush that ran straight across the building. There was something about the long, low, wide house that was not sufficiently imposing for the formality of formal gardens,

[166]

of gravelled walks that threaded under arbors and led to swimming-pool and lily-pond. Flash of white-flanked garden statuary. Satyrs on pedestals behind flame of hydrangea. Flower-beds the shape and colour of fast pinwheels.

It was rather as if the house was a not quite precious jewel, magnificently mounted. Probably because, by contrast, there was a procession of Renaissance, Colonial, and Tudor magnificences perched along that particular section of Hudson River frontage. The Rhincoop place. Herbert Wing's. The Italian palace of the Judge.

Gleam of their turrets through trees. Long driveways overhung with elms and willows that completely concealed porticos, striped awnings, tennis-courts, and correspondingly Renaissance or Tudor litter of garages, toolhouses, and lodges.

Yet in a way Martin loved the inadequacy of the Georgian house, set too low in the magnificence of its surroundings. It took some of the edge off the granite magnificence that surrounded Max Innesbrook even when he sat in his mahogany and Maxfield Parrish office in Park Row and pressed buttons.

The button-pressing Max Innesbrook. He punctuated his talk with pressure of buttons when a thought would invade his conversation that was relevant to something else. Max Innesbrook could talk tariff and think tacks; discuss Egyptian scarabs, of which he owned the first and largest individual collection in the world, and press a button for a clerk to summon a calciminer to come and take an order to do over the chicken-roost for his prize Leghorns.

The button-pressing Max Innesbrook, releasing by the touch of a finger this and that dam of energy under his control.

The pressing of buttons. Sometimes it seemed to Martin that they were just so many human eyes in a row beside him, waiting to be gouged.

The rather homey, homely house that Max Innesbrook was rich enough to dare, mitigated a bit the grandeur of the Innesbrook manner.

There was a carpet hassock, the kind Martin remembered in his father's threadbare house on the campus of Northwestern University, under the dining-room table for the limited reach of his Aunt Emma's stodgy legs. Squat, piano-looking legs that made her appear so much shorter from the waist down than from the waist up. Martin loved the persistence of that old hassock through the overbearing kind of Tudor dining-room splendour. It gave him the reassurance that certain inadequacies of his Aunt Emma always gave him. The fact that her jabots would never stay straight. The fact that she was always trailing something and stooping for it with a grunt. A ball of wool. A ripped flounce. And there was something absurdly reassuring, as against the granite solidarity of his uncle, in the fact that all three of the Innesbrook girls had protruding teeth. A rushing formation of long white ones, peculiar to neither parent, which thrust out the girls' upper lips like awnings.

It did not seem to matter that a razor-blade king of social-register standing occupied the grey stone château opposite, or that the adjoining estate of a highly eminent judge and his wife was an authentic copy of the Villa d'Este.

His aunt Emma and the girls in the midst of magnificence were strangely reminiscent to Martin of the Iowa town in which he had spent the first sixteen years of his life. The odour of Keokuk lurked in that house. And a coziness. Coziness of hassock, knitting-needles, and firelight. Doughnuts with powdered sugar at tea-time. The rather ominous coziness of three spinsters and an over-anxious mother.

Martin could talk to these women kinfolk of his. He could lie stretched on the lawn, outrageous young egoist, all of a Saturday afternoon after a tennis tilt with one of the girls or a walk with his aunt, berating the impregnability of his uncle, sketching his dreams, tilting at his windmills.

It was when the grey mediæval-looking pile of Max Innesbrook himself arrived upon the scene that the something in Martin could seem to stop as if his veins were frozen pipes.

Not that his uncle ever literally arrived on any scene. He was the kind of person who could always seem ensconced. In office. In conference. In his library. In the glassed-in veranda he called study.

Ensconced, with a frieze of figures in an ante-room, awaiting appointment with him.

And the push-buttons! The rows of them upon which he played constantly, as if they were organ stops.

The granite power of Max Innesbrook. He was squint-eyed with it.

He never regarded young Innesbrook except with that squint at its tightest. Even when they met at parchesi, week-ends, and at table or in the gymnasium where Max Innesbrook took his exercise on a stationary bicycle enclosed in an electric bath-cabinet.

And then, in the way of any close contacts with this curious silent man entrenched behind the bulwarks of his push-buttons, there were always such various impedimenta as visiting Norwegian explorers, British novelists, foreign ambassadors, eminent scientists, poets, composers, capitalists.

There was no getting him alone, except sometimes in the gymnasium over the garage, when the great man, his head swathed in Turkish towels, emerged from the cabinet which contained the ludicrous spectacle of bony austere legs riding the bicycle to nowhere.

Max Innesbrook loathed exercise. It bored him. There were always books, magazines, newspapers, budgets, schedules, itineraries, and reports propped up on top of the cabinet to be read as he pedalled. Martin had long since figured out that the best place to beard his uncle was in the den of his gymnasium.

In fact the only talks they ever had took place there.

Max Innesbrook, like a Roman senator with a Turkish towel for toga, squinting at his nephew perched in enviable straddle of youth across a leather "horse."

Egoist! Opinionated young simpleton. Vacillating as his father. Conceited young carp. Uplifter, with more ego than sincerity. Writings full of bombast. I started out on a rival sheet when my father ran the best newspaper in Keokuk. Got by on my own gumption. Let him show me his.

The morning that Martin arrived at Innesbrook for the week-end with an article entitled "The Blameless Sex" and the beginning of a second in his brief-case, he paid his respects to his aunt and the wife of a visiting Spanish painter, out taking snap-shots of each other along the hydrangea border which divided their gardens from the sunken ones of the Judge, and then made a bee-line for the gymnasium.

"Morning, Uncle. Your favourite nephew and prodigy journalist salutes you!"

"Umph. Tell that black nigger to turn off a few of those lamps. There's a noise down there around the pedals like I'm frying."

"You've the right idea on that McClasky case, Uncle. Now my idea of the force of an editorial like yours this morning ——"

"Will never set the world on fire. A *few* of those lamps, George, I said. Not all. Dunderhead, not all! Turn on the upper row around my waistband. That's where I can do with a little concentrated electricity."

"As a matter of fact, I suppose those in the know, Uncle, realize that the entire decision in the McClasky case rested on you."

"Umph! Hang that dunderhead! Didn't I say all those lights? What the devil is he trying to do? Turn this into an incinerator? Umph. That's better. Press that third button, second row. Why the devil don't that fellow Halsey answer a ring when he gets it? Halsey, wire Cleveland and say that MacGowen will take up the matter of those new presses with the Detroit offices. Telephone MacGowen and tell him to catch the Wolverine out for Detroit to-day. 'S all.''

"Now, if I had your power, Uncle ——"

"Idle speculation."

"Not a bit of it. The reason you don't regard me as a nephew prodigy, Uncle, is because just an ordinary above-the-average brain like mine doesn't mean anything to you. You surround yourself with them at fifty thousand per. You buy brains. Picked ones, like mine, except when they happen to be right in the family. Heretofore I've just presented you with the usual fifty-thousand-dollar brand of clear thinking. That's about all those articles of mine, that you have read, can boast of. Clear thinking."

"I've never read one worth a boast. In fact, don't know's I've read any at all."

"Delighted to hear you're in some doubt on the subject."

"Hang that nigger! Where is he? Hey, off with those lights around my waist-line. I'm not competing with Madame Polari. You were wrong in your conclusions about the MacClasky editorial. Good journalism, but bad logic."

"I see where you're going lightly on the Scott acquittal."

"Bah! That woman's guilty as hell."

"And then they say the woman pays."

"Poppycock. Her sex is what saved her from the chair!"

"I say, Uncle, you've hit something there. By Jove, your mind works like a trigger! There is no such thing as sexless justice in this country! Queer nobody's sized it up that way before."

"Tell that black scalawag to let me out of here before I begin to fry!"

"Yes, sir, Uncle, you're one hundred per cent. right. Directly on top of the emancipation of women comes the greatest murder wave in the history of the country, and not a male jury will convict one! Look at the Scott case! Just as you say, her sex is what saved her from the chair. Then there's the Ellington case. The Trentini girl. That Idiola murder. Guilty as hell, every one of them! In this country to-day women can literally get away with murder.

Sexless Justice. Blameless sex. Even I could
do you a couple of smashing articles based on
your idea. Great stuff, Uncle. Your mind
works like a dynamo."

"Call that nigger," said Max Innesbrook.
"Turn on my shower, George. And hey, you.
You! Martin. Press that third button. Halsey, come stand on the outside of the rubber
curtain while I have my shower and take a
letter. Dang that nigger, where'd he put my
specs? Ready? Take a letter. See that Mr.
Innesbrook has it before he leaves the house.
And you, Martin, take the letter that Halsey
gives you and hand it to Robinson to-morrow
at nine. Report to him for a desk job. Details
later. Dang that nigger, where's the soap?"

*

May-day came on a Saturday. May-days
seemed to have a habit of being auspicious for
Orchid. There was the memory of a dim and
sooty May-day in Mulberry Street. Nana with
her lye-bitten hands at the making of a pink
tissue paper dress. Nana. Water under bridges
at night. Barges that sink, keel up. She could
never pass a wharf at night, or the silhouette of
women who scrub floors or lurk in doorways,
without that gnarled image crossing her memory. Nana, whom she had called mother.

Memory of her lay in the heart like a cloud. The derelict of a hat with the pulp of rose mashed into the crown was a grim object that Orchid kept pinned in a towel and hidden away in the bottom of her trunk. Nana. It was in keeping with her life, somehow, that the waters of oblivion should literally have sucked her down.

Yes, May-days had a habit of being auspicious for Orchid. It was on a May-day that she had been called to take the place of Leland Deland.

This May-day, however, was the most gala of them all. The Franco-American Fashion Convention was on. She had been one of a half-dozen picked mannequins, from various importing firms, who had been sent to "show" at the Belvedere in Philadelphia and the Copley in Boston.

Martin had teased her about all the rotogravures of her in the Sunday sections, along with the ostrich mother of triplets, Mrs. Hamilton Stuyvesant on the links at Lenox, and an Australian diver in his two-rooms-and-kitchenette helmet.

On May-day the International Convention closed its session with the season's most important fashion-show at the Ritz.

The plums had fallen to Orchid; the Frisby

MANNEQUIN

Sœurs and Corinne models, which she wore particularly well, and also some of the sports togs from Cleo, that by heretofore indisputable right had been worn by Cyd. She tried to placate her with lunch at Henri's. As a matter of fact, she would gladly have foregone the sports togs entirely. But Cyd would not be placated. Nor Toto, nor Denise. Orchid was the only model from Drecotte's exhibiting that day. There was only one mannequin from each firm, and selection was a matter beyond the control of anyone except Sam Mandel himself. But that fact seemed to have no mitigating effect upon the girls. The lips of Cyd were as twisted as if they had been wrung.

It bothered and depressed Orchid. She even volunteered to Sam Mandel, who would have none of the arrangement, to alternate with the girls. But once on the platform and down the runway, in the fabrics that lay to her flesh like petals, it was sweet, even with the background of envy and bitterness, to feel the little shimmer of success.

Soft rush of summer furs. A canary-coloured shadow-lace frock named Topaz, from Jeanne et Fils, with garden hat of the shadow-lace and one huge Easter lily laid across the brim. A grey-and-violet dinner dress from Tonie and Toinette, with a two-yard trail of tulle sash.

Drecotte's "Nile," a black velvet, daringly low, and with the chic absurdity of sleeves that reached from wrist to elbow. Moret's famous model of the season, "Magnolia." Quick sheath of tight-wrapped cream velvet, unrelieved except for the large rhinestone butterfly that fastened to the bare left shoulder-blade by means of a tiny suction-cup.

The Oh's and the Ah's came up like powder off a puff when she appeared in that; and then a pleasant turmoil of applause. She stood on the runway. She held out her arms with the gesture of a giant imperator moth trying its wings. She revolved with a slow statuesque rhythm.

But Martin liked best the last frock. And so, judging from the swell of applause, did the audience that jammed the ballroom. "Ariel," from Suzanne Longchamps. Ariel, doubtless, because it was a pale sort of moon-and-mist thing, so sheer that the underslip of faint blue embroidered chiffon came through the flesh-pink organdie in all its minute design, like frost-tracery on a window-pane. It was outrageously bouffé and frivolous, and in a way that the French can be bouffé and frivolous.

There was a garden hat, too, with a band of pink chiffon that came down and half veiled the eyes; and then, in the same bouffant mood, a toreador cape of the pink chiffon paradoxically edged in a deep border of blue fox and fastened on the left shoulder with a jewelled dagger of gilt filigree and rose quartz.

"Ariel. Garden costume. Suzanne Longchamps," said the catalogue, and there was a special curtain-drop for it, of clipped hedge, gleam of statuary, curve of fountain.

"You know what!" exclaimed Martin immediately after the show, regarding her as if he could not leave off looking, and his hair with the furrows through it down in a damp peak over his right brow. "Know what? Shame for you not to have a real garden party to show off that rig, on this day of garden parties. Say, here's an idea! It's May-day fête up in Westchester, and there's a four-in-one fête at Innesbrook. Four estates thrown into one for the garden party. Annual performance. All the social Choctaws and their squaws. I was going up in the train. Promised my cousin. On the prospect of my first week's salary on my new job, I'll hire a taxi and take you up with me!"

"Martin! The May-day fête at Marblestone! Me?"

Impulsive Martin. Almost immediately the beet-red of wanting to recall his words gushed across his face. Hang it, one of those impulsive jams he was always getting himself in for. Hang it, that wasn't the way he wanted Orchid to dawn upon his relatives. Togs. Togs. Glad when the day came that she would never have to parade another one of them. Not that he had any of the stale reactionary inhibitions about women and jobs, but just the same, hang that tongue of his! There was the last of a series of articles he was doing that had to be finished by midnight. Of course it was practically blocked out, but a fellow had to crash through big in order to even make a dent with a man like Max Innesbrook. Besides, it would have been more fun to chuck the Innesbrook idea anyway, remain in town, and have a bite of dinner with Orchid at the Antique. Then to the office at a decent hour and finish the article. Unnecessary explanations, taking her out there in this fashion. Too soon to spring Orchid on the family. Plenty of time for that row. Hang!

Martin standing there chewing his lip as if for having betrayed him into the impulsive outburst. And Orchid so unmistakably eager, there in the garden-party dress that was lovely as mist around her.

"Oh, Martin!"

"You want to go, Orchid?"

"Do I? I've never been anywhere really

beautiful, Martin. If Mr. Mandel here doesn't care — if you and Mr. Mandel are ——"

"If Mr. Mandel doesn't care? Say, believe me, it's worth the price of the outfit you should show yourself in something from Drecotte on such an occasion like the Marblestone Fête. Just to show you how all right it is with me, I'll send you out in my car."

"Mr. Mandel!"

Poor Martin. His damp forelock made him look all the helplessness he felt. Of course if Orchid wanted to go, poor little thing. Of course, natural she should want to. Blamed impulsive thing, though, for him to have blurted out. Couldn't very well disappoint her now. Last year's fête was a beastly bore. Doubtless the same this year. But, of course, since Orchid had her heart set on going ——

"I guess I shouldn't, but oh! Martin, I do want to go — if — if it's all right that I should. If you really mean it."

"Surely I do. Thank you, Mr. Mandel, for the car. We'll be back before seven. Don't mind having to return early, do you, Orchid? I've an article to get in, you know. Midnight deadline. We'll just hike out for a look-in and right back."

"Martin, you're a darling!"

*

For the first time, on the ride to Innesbrook that day of blue sky, pink clouds, and warm taste of spring, Martin and Orchid dared to plan.

It was the May wine of air, of strawberry-coloured clouds, and the whiff of sachet in chiffon, that must have made them a little heady. The two of them. Martin, who did not even know what his cheque-envelope would contain at the end of the first week of his new desk position, off on his first half-holiday as if the afternoon were an eternity and eternity were spring.

Martin, dear silliness, counting his eggs even before the first of them was hatched.

Martin, dear silliness, wanted a house with a gabled roof that tied under its chin like an old witch's cap. And Dutch blue hearth-tiles. And a laundry-chute! He was not quite clear about the chute, because the house was to be a one-storey affair; but all his life, Martin declared, he had wanted a laundry-chute. Not that he had ever seen one, but, willy-nilly, silly-billy, Martin wanted a laundry-chute. Suddenly, in the key of being absolutely irresponsible, Orchid wanted one too. The laundry-chute in her and Martin's house that tied under its chin. The end of the week would tell the tale. Orchid was so sure. Martin was so sure. If Martin's envelope contained as little as forty dollars, they were going to take the leap. Over the precipice and into the garden of the house that tied under its chin. On less than the forty if need be. At least, Orchid was willing to leap on less than that. Finally she beat Martin down to thirty-five.

What did it matter that Orchid's original dreams had not to do exactly with gabled roofs? Just Martin wanting it, somewhere within commuting distance of Park Row, and on a slope with what he called a double chin of terrace, and, of course, the darling laundry-chute, made it seem suddenly more desired than anything else could be.

More desired than her own dream. An old dream. There was a handsome book of prints in one of the architectural rooms at the Public Library, where sometimes she escaped at lunch-hour from the crowded room with Toto and Myrrh and Cyd. Reproductions of old-world beauty spots of art and architecture were in that book. The librarian in the department, who came to know her, would unlock a glass case and lift it out for her. Interior view of the Palace of the Duke d'Abruzzi, seventeenth century. Florence. Prince Vallombrosa's summer home in Venice. Late sixteenth century. Façade of Uffizi Gallery, Florence. Doors of

MANNEQUIN

Giotto's Campanile. Mellow old beauty of Credenzas. Savonarola chairs in gold fringe and red velvets. Triptychs with mediæval madonnas fading into the wood. Refectory tables. Bench and beam and Gothic arch. Those had been part of her dream until Martin upset it with his whimsical one of the house that was to look like an old woman with a cap that tied under her chin.

It made necessary the putting-aside of the old dreams. The patinas of mellow wood. Fabrics made lustrous with the mysterious laying-on of the hands of time. Often, Saturday afternoons, puttering around antique- and second-hand shops, and sometimes auction rooms, she could browse and finger for hours among old bits of Spanish and Venetian brocades and laces, just for the feel of them.

And now dear Martin, with his adorable boyish nonsense of the house that tied under the chin. Compromise became a joy.

"But cripes! Orchid, what frightens me is that at heart you're such a stickler for everything snooty. It's right that you should be, of course. But you should have picked out some fellow with a million dollars spending-money in his pocket. Nobody could sit there in that rig of yours and look the dyed-in-the-wool, blown-in-the-glass, hot-house Orchid that you do and not deserve to be snooty. That's why the forty bucks a week frightens me."

"Martin, you talk as if poverty were new to me; as if my entire life has been anything except a struggle against the darkest brand of it."

"That's just it. I want your married life to atone for all that. I don't want the odds to continue against you."

"But, Martin dear, with you there will be no odds. How little you understand that side of me. My training has developed in me a genius for making something out of nothing. If I can't have the Italian palace I visualize when I get the sillies and start seeing things, I'll make our witch's house daintier than anything you ever imagined. And on your forty a week, too. On *our* forty a week."

"Dearest dear, I love you for saying that. Only why the devil am I bringing you up here to this fête to see all the things we won't be able to afford? Once you clap eyes on the Judge's place, it's apt to knock our witch's house higher'n a cocked hat."

"I love the idea of starting in a gingerbread witch's house."

"That's it, sweetheart! it only means a start. Mark my word, Orchid, I've got enough of my uncle in me to duplicate all over again his kind of success. Only plus! My way. The way not merely of big journalism but of big idealism. Forward-looking journalism. Bet on me, Orchid. I'll win."

"I wouldn't bet on a sure thing, Martin."

"You dearest ever."

"That's what you are, Martin. The dearest ever."

Hand in Martin's, there in the gliding rush of Sam Mandel's mauve limousine, the May wine of spring was against their lips, as they met.

*

And then, when they turned down an aisle of trees that formed an arch over a gravel drive that seemed to be leading into an ocean of hydrangeas, stage-fright set in.

"Martin, I — I feel like — like something stuffed — a doll with the sawdust running out. Martin, have the chauffeur turn back, please. I can't face it. I shouldn't have let you bring me. You had the good sense to want to renig at the start. I should have had, too. I'm out of my depth, dear. Please!"

"Hear, hear!"

"What's that? Music? They must be dancing over in that flag-draped pavilion. I've never in my life been on a dance-floor. Please,

Martin, I forced you to bring me, but I was a pig. You've an article to do to-night, Martin. Let's turn back ——''

"Nothing like that, my pretty lady. Besides, Miss Adrienne, my aunt's cock-eyed secretary, has already seen us. You wanted to come, and now that I have you here I don't intend to be cheated out of the thrill of arriving with the only girl I've ever seen in my life who really looked the rôle of Queen of the May."

"Martin, is that your uncle's house there through the trees?"

"No, that's the Herrick place. I'll take you over there later, and to the Wings' too. All the adjoining estates are thrown open to-day. Herrick's is about the show-place of whole Westchester, I guess. Villa d'Este to the life, they say. I've never been to Italy, and I can't even remember the look of the original from the picture post-cards. That's how wise I am on period stuff. But you ought to enjoy it, Orchid. It's your kind of thing. Ever heard of Judge Herrick? Of course you have."

"What figure is that, Martin, there against that heavenly semi-circle of green hedge?"

"That's Eros, my fair one, standing there labouring under the delusion that we need any-one to shoot a love-dart at us."

"Eros." Another mental note for a trip to the reference-room.

"Martin, those flaming lovely things?"

"Dahlias. Mrs. Herrick goes in for them."

"Oh. Ah. Ah!"

"From here on, now, we're on my uncle's place. See that house with the tower on one end like a swollen jaw?"

"Martin, I'm frightened. Those tables under the trees! Are we supposed to eat and drink? Martin, oh, Martin, look, over on the Herricks' side. It can't be real. Martin, a white peacock! A green terrace and white marble steps and lily-pond and white peacocks!"

"That's nothing. Wait until you see the Herrick Roman gardens, and, on down below their place, the Wing terraces. My uncle's place is not much on sunken gardens and poppycock architecture, but pretty nice grounds, aren't they? And that's his gym up there over the garage. Holy old terror! That's where I beard the lion in his den."

"Martin, it's all too lovely. Let's drive back, to the Antique for dinner. Martin, I'm frightened."

"Too late. Here we are. Stick by me. My favourite rôle at these shindigs is to hover lovingly on the edge of the chicken salad and the punch and then do a well-fed fade-out."

[188]

MANNEQUIN

There was remotely pleasant music, from a group of native Hawaiians in yellow paper necklaces, and in the slanting light of afternoon the gayety of figures moving against green terraces. Men in flannels and women in coloured splash of frock and parasol.

"Martin," whispered Orchid, and dug with her nails into his wrist, "don't leave me even for an instant."

"Hi there, Aunt Em. Hi, wait a minute. It's me, or I, whichever puts me in the right. Want you to meet a friend of mine, Aunt Em. Miss Sargossa, my aunt Mrs. Innesbrook. Orchid, want you to meet my three cousins."

For the life of Martin he could not keep down his pride. The pride of possession. Pride in the stares of his aunt and his cousins, and then more stares from groups that strolled up. Stares at the loveliness of Orchid. The lovelinesss that belonged to him.

"Has Martin shown you the grounds, Miss Sargossa? Martin, take Miss Sargossa over to meet your uncle, although I suppose, as usual, he is nowhere to be found. Probably hidden in his study. Give her some food, Martin, and show her about. Some of the guests are finding it rather amusing to ride over to the Wings' in the pony phaetons you'll find near the greenhouses. Do make yourself at home,

Miss — Miss — Sargossa. So nice of Martin to have brought you. Bad boy, you, where were you on Friday when you promised your cousin Celeste to come out for tennis?"

"Good Lord, Aunt Em, I forgot. Celeste, oh, I say, Celeste, let me explain."

These gracious people. They made the new world seem not so remote after all.

"Martin, everybody — is staring so —— Stay with me, Martin."

"Of course they're staring. Funny thing, instead of making me mad as hops it makes me proud as hops. Old reactionary idea, that a fellow resents public admiration of the woman he's in love with. Hang it, I'm proud of you. You're the stunningest thing that has ever been let loose at one of these solemn fests before. Mark Delano wants to meet you so badly he's screwing his face into pleats."

"Martin, not *the* Mark Delano?"

"Hi, Mark, want you to meet Miss Sargossa. Mr. and Mrs. Delano. Yes, one and the same. You've probably read some of his stuff. Pretty bad reading, but pretty good selling. Aren't I right, you old robber, you?"

Mark Delano himself! Even Martin, contemptuous of most contemporary fiction, put Mark Delano on his reading-list for Orchid. Mark Delano! A paunchy little man, very much in the flesh, and a grey-haired woman who dragged at his arm like a bit of seaweed, his wife.

"Hello, Jelenko! Want you to meet Miss Sargossa. Nope, sorry, old man, but I'm taking her around myself. Orchid, beware of that pirate. He goes off and finds North Poles and things and is full of the instinct to carry off anything he sees that he wants."

"Not C. J. Jelenko, Martin?"

"None other, nasty tennis arm and all, with which he once licked me to smithereens on these very courts. See you later, old man. Preferably at the North Pole. No, nothing doing. Told you I was doing my own personal conducting this afternoon. Get that. Personal. Old pirate, you."

"Martin, it's like Who's Who come to life."

"Yes, but all the 'Who's Who' is about you. Look at them. Dear little old dear, you've got them guessing."

"Martin, hadn't you better just be frank about it? These clothes — me — just tell them, dear, the truth. One or two knowing that I'm a dressmaker's model with a half-day off will be enough to spread the glad tidings. Sad-but-true. Please, Martin, hadn't you better?"

"Sure I had. Nothing to hide. Watch!

Mr. Stroheim! How do you do, Mrs. Stroheim. Want you both to meet Miss Orchid Sargossa. Mr. Stroheim, Miss Sargossa is with Drecotte. Sometime I want to bring her down to your French rooms."

"Martin, Martin, not Stroheim Brothers' Department Store?"

"None other."

"Miss Sargossa has been showing this afternoon at the Ritz. Knew you two would be interested in duds. S'long."

Dear Martin, to have been so easy and frank about it and to have taken the onus off the false pretences of the gorgeousness of the garden costume.

"Martin, you're a darling. Now everyone will know. Hadn't you better, though, run back and personally explain to your aunt?"

"Aunt Em? What does she care whether ——"

"I know, Martin, I know. But just the same, I wish you would."

"All right, if it will make you feel any better. Sit and wait here on this marble bench and don't look as if you are afraid that somebody's going to bite you. Nobody is, except possibly Mark Delano, who looks as if he would like to eat you with a spoon. Or I, because I love you."

MANNEQUIN

The Delanos strolled up while Martin was
gone. And a Mr. and Mrs. Herbert Wing, a
shaggy fellow with an ash-grey wife in long
pendant earrings. It was incredible, sitting
there talking with them. Of spring in Westchester. The colour of Bougainvillæa, which
Delano described in the short snatchy fashion
he had of talking. White collies, apropos of the
wolfhound at Mrs. Wing's side. More people
strolled up into quite a group. Pleasurable excitement mounted. No one was going to snub
her. One of the men even asked her about Sam
Mandel of Drecotte. Herbert Wing handed
her an ice and commented on the rose quartz
shoulder dagger she wore, describing a Chinese
amethyst he was having mounted for his wife.
No one was going to snub her. Only, there
was creeping over her a consciousness that to
these people there was something about her of
a side-show in a tent.

Beautiful dressmaker's model. Well-known
mannequin. Young Innesbrook hitting the
high spots. Allen Terry strolled up. Indeed
she remembered him. With all her repugnance.

"Had the pleasure," he said laconically to
Delano's introduction, and seated himself on
the stone bench beside her.

"Well, small world, isn't it?"

"Yes."

[193]

"Had some fodder?"

"Some what!"

"Chicken salad and cold cream dressing. Fruit punch, all fruit and no punch."

"Yes, thank you, I've had."

"If you really want a bracer, I'll drive you over to my place. Only ten minutes from here."

"No, thank you."

"Well, there ought to be something decently wet over at the Rhincoop place, or at Wing's, for that matter. Want to get into one of those phaeton things and wobble over? They're supposed to be *au fait* at these morgue fêtes."

"No, thank you."

"You're gorgeous."

"Everything out here is."

"Rot. 'Afternoon of the Octogenarians,' is what I call these annuals. It will liven up after supper on the lawns. The wine-cellars then yield up their keys. What are you doing here? Exhibiting?"

"In — a — way; I mean, if you put it that way, I — I guess I am. I came with a friend."

"Meouw. Come on, I'll show you around."

"Please, I said no."

To her enormous relief Martin came up just then.

"Howdy, Allen. Come, Orchid, let's take

the pony express over to the Herricks'. See you later, Terry. Didn't mind running into him out here, did you, honey?"

"No, Martin, only it was blessed when you came along. You dear, you!"

"Rat, that's what he is. Look, Orchid, there are some of your namesakes growing under glass. Mrs. Herrick goes in for them. You *are* like them, Orchid, honestly. Cool. Fastidious. A little bit remote."

"Martin, silly dear, never to you."

"No, dear, hardly ever."

There was a flight of marble steps from the Herrick terrace to a square lily-pond lined in green tiles that gave the water iridescence. And there against the gleam of terrace was the white peacock, strutting up.

"Good Lord, Ork," whispered Martin, "don't stand there yammering at that peacock. They're all looking at us. I mean at you. The whole world is looking at you. The whole universe. Why in blazes didn't I go home and at least climb out of these old tweeds into flannels?"

"Martin, please don't drag me so!"

"There's the Judge now, up in that little loggia talking to old man Rhincoop. I want you to know Judge Herrick, Orchid; he's a really great person."

"Martin, please, not so fast. I'm frightened."

"Silly. He's such a simple person that I am sure he is the one most apt to be frightened. That's his wife to the left, with all those young girls around her. The good-looking woman with the marcelled white hair. She dotes on girls. She was a nervous wreck for years, about some kind of a happening. Forget what it was. Years ago. Want you to meet her, too. She's your kind."

"What do you mean, Martin, by my kind?"

"Oh no you don't! That doesn't work. I see through your ruse of trying to engage me in polite conversation by sitting yourself down on this bench to ward off the evil moment. Orchid, I didn't know you were shy!"

"But what do you really mean, Martin, by my kind?"

"Oh, just this kind of thing. Love of beauty. All this estate is her doing. The Judge would just as soon live in a log cabin. But she's like you, Orchid. She's an exotic. That's why forty dollars a week gives me the nervous hydrophobia, although from what I understand she and the Judge started on less."

"Martin, she's beautiful."

"Who?"

"Mrs. Herrick. And what a solemn sort of person he looks."

"Yes. Whenever I want to rag my uncle I tell him there's one judge living not a thousand miles away from him who would not allow himself to be railroaded by the Innesbrook dynasty. Touchy spot with the old gentleman. Come on, I want you to meet the Judge. Stop playing the timorous puss rôle now, and behave, or papa'll spank. Judge Herrick, I want you to meet my — I want you to meet someone who is standing absolutely speechless from being impressed by your greatness. Judge Herrick, this is Miss Sargossa."

His eyes were kind. Amused clear eyes.

"Bless your heart, you just about took the breath of this party away by the picture you made arriving. Even with you in, young scamp, to spoil it. Mrs. Herrick wants to meet you. Selene, this is Miss Sargossa, a friend of Innesbrook's."

"I wonder if you realize how lovely you were coming down those steps, Miss Sargossa. Of course you don't. That was part of the picture."

Poor Orchid, her mouth was like a rusk; full of tongue that felt swollen. And her eyes two hot stinging pains.

"You — you're beautiful."

MANNEQUIN

It was the supremely foolish thing to say. She knew it as she felt the words coming. And Martin knew it, too, and, to help her, broke into nervous staccato conversation.

"Miss Sargossa is a lover of your sort of thing, Mrs. Herrick. She's just in the common ordinary everyday dressmaking business herself, but she's keen on the Spanish and the Italian sort of thing in furniture and architecture. Now, I was telling her on the drive out that my idea of the perfect interior is the Salem Witch period."

"Martin!"

"If what Martin says about you is true, make up your mind to be a helpless victim to my hobby. I'd love showing you my house."

"Oh — if you would!"

"Martin, you stay out here and see that the Judge toes the mark as host. Miss Sargossa and I are going snooping. Woe unto anyone who shows herself sympathetic to my love of things. I remember, as a young married woman when we were just starting out, my husband always used to say, 'Beware that love of things doesn't smother you like the falling of bracelets and shields in the old Greek story.' But really, I don't think they have succeeded in smothering me, Miss Sargossa. They have only made the world seem a lovelier place."

Poor Orchid. She wanted to put out her hand on the forearm of Selene Herrick, because it was bare and because almost beyond any desire she had ever experienced she wanted to touch it.

"I — are you sure you have the time to — to show me around now? All your guests ——"

"Wait until you know me better, dear, and you'll understand that I have time for anybody who loves my things as I love them. Come, we'll start from this end. This is the loggia. It's a direct reproduction, you see, of the Villa d'Este. Ever seen it? Well, you will some day. My husband took me there while I was recovering from a long and severe nervous breakdown, and I vowed then that I would never be satisfied with anything less than a Villa d'Este of my own. I want to call your attention to these fluted arches. After one has lost interest in life as I did, my dear, for seven long years, well, I suppose any average husband, much less the best of them, like mine, would be glad to gratify such a whim if it were in his power. All my life I've loved the kind of things that belonged to seventeenth- and eighteenth-century Italy and Spain."

Orchid, with her limited knowledge of even

the phraseology of the things she loved, standing dumb there among them.

There were stone halls padded in rugs that felt high as the nap of fur to the feet, and stairways with tile and mosaic done into the stonework. And a cloistered courtyard into which the sun flowed, but which was austere with imported Italian cypress-trees and the kind of perspective that reminded one of the prints of Dante walking against Italian dusks, that hung in the art department of the Titanic.

Bedrooms in ascetic Gothic magnificence. Black oak bedsteads of priceless patina and spread with the old red brocatelles that had made the seventeenth century glow. Faïence-encrusted goblets. Wood carvings with decay at them. A gold-brocaded chasuble from a Medici salon across one wall of the dining-room. Churchly windows with the light streaming through stained glass.

Corridors of doors. Gothic doors with entire incidents from the Old Testament carved against them. Doors that led down steps, around corners, and into Pompeian bathrooms done in black marble and gold-and-red friezes. Solariums. A library with an organ across one end of it.

A magnificent walnut door with a wrought-iron lock.

MANNEQUIN

"That door," said Mrs. Herrick, passing it, "opens into the sunniest room in the house. An empty room. A waiting, empty room."

"A what?"

"The empty, sunlit, waiting room, I used to call it, until it made my husband angry."

"What beautiful doors! I don't know exactly how to describe it — all this — but just seeing it is as if, as if an ache you never quite knew you had, had suddenly been cured."

"That's exactly the way I feel. My beautiful things soothe me. They even, in their inanimate way, make up for the — the cruel things that can sometimes make life almost unbearable."

"If I lived here, I don't know, I — I don't know ——"

"You nice girl, I wish you did."

"And you've a patio! All my life I've dreamed of a patio. They have one in the House Beautiful in the furniture department at Stroheim's. Fountain, trellises, and all! Have you ever been in the Spanish house there? I love to wander through it. But of course to you theirs would be just second-rate."

"Why, yes, rather. But there was a time when that kind of thing delighted me, too. My dear, you *are* lovely, standing there against

that western light. You don't mind my saying so, do you?"

"How could I? I, too, think you're lovely."

"How beautifully you wear those sheer
things."

"They aren't mine, you know. I model."

"I see. I should think you would be a great
success. That ornament! How cunning! It
has the effect of plunging right through your
shoulder."

"After a day in and out of a costume like
this, that's exactly what it seems to do around
going-home time."

"I wonder if you would like to see my
hot-house. My own little private one of orchids."

"My name is Orchid."

"How lovely! Now that you mention it,
really you are like one. Your mother must
have loved them and seen some of their beauty
in you."

"I — er — yes——"

"Here we are. Jones, roll back those awnings. I want to show those speckled ones.
They are extremely rare. In fact, my husband
sent all the way to Tangiers for the cuts.
But it's the lavenders and mauves I love best.
Jones, cut a corsage of lavendar and pink ones
for Miss Sargossa."

MANNEQUIN

"Mrs. Herrick, you mustn't give me so much of your time. Your guests will be wondering."

"I can't begin to tell you how wonderful it has been, dear girl, showing you my hobbies. Somehow, it's almost as if you were one of my hobbies arriving just now in the lovely crate of that orchid-coloured gown. I'm afraid I'm a hopeless girl-addict. I love them. Come, we had better go back; but I won't let you run away from me."

To Orchid, standing once more on the terrace, the soft swirl of fête around her, tinkle of laughter and fountains and punch-glasses, it was as if, just as the model gown fitted her proportions, so this environment was something that she slid into so naturally; something that somehow was not even new to her; something that was hers, always had been.

The Judge and the explorer bandied about with her, besting her in repartee, which caused the Judge to pinch her cheek when it flushed and tilt her head back to see if he had teased tears into her eyes.

If the young girls were stand-offish and a little cruel in their air of seeming to patronize, it was the kind of patronage that, even as it cut in, poured balm into the wound. The patronage of hurt vanities.

"Martin's brought a dressmaker's model. A bit nervy of him, I'll say. My dear, observe the men! Wonder if they know how funny they are. My dears, we are rank amateurs. This is professional day. The only way to really break into Westchester for sure is to arrive in a hired Longchamps model and feed white peacocks on the terrace. Wish you'd look at Allen Terry. My dears, he'll fall in the honey-pot if he isn't careful. Of course she would be his pace. But I didn't know that Martin went in for them, too!"

It *was* annoying. Allen Terry, buzzing about so, had to be brushed off constantly, like a fly.

"Come on, this affair's got sleeping-sickness. I'll drive you over to my place. You must be dry."

"Please, I've told you no!"

"As you will. If you can stand it, I can."

There was always a little swirl about Orchid. It was pleasant while the Judge and Mrs. Herrick were by. Actually people were wanting to meet her. The women with close eyes of scrutiny as they came face to face, but the men in frank groups of waiting their turn and wanting to dance attendance.

If only Allen Terry wouldn't buzz so. And there were the Herricks going off with a newly arrived French diplomat and his wife toward the refreshment pergola. Martin shouldn't have left her alone like this. He must be closeted with his uncle. Young Terry at her elbow, bringing her sandwiches and purple punch that he made run over the sides of the glass because he was always insisting upon pouring into it something from a silver hip-flask that made it bitter.

"No likee," she said, and smiled up at him through a wry crinkling nose.

"It's liquid fire distilled out of opals," he said, and took a draught of it in the raw.

If only he wouldn't hover so, with his liquid fire distilled from opals.

Martin routed him all right when he did appear. "Clear out, old man. Programme filled. Here's a peace-offering. A box of my uncle's private brand of cigarettes. They'll make a strong man weep. Any tennis this year? Good."

That was clever of Martin. Wanting to keep peace and walking away on his arm, Orchid snuggled herself a little into his elbow.

"You darling, I feel like you've been gone for years."

"The old man's giving the first of my series to-morrow morning release. Wish it were midnight. We can get the Sunday edition by then. Want to see how it sets up. Old man don't say much, but I think he's sold on it. Come on, I'm so full of it all I want to get back now and bone down to work."

Of course. Of course. But it did seem so early. So almost cruelly early. The sky, cool now of its sunset fires, and a first star leaping out. There was to be supper on the lawn. Waiters scurried with planks that fitted over wooden horses and formed long picnic-tables. There were whole hams stuck all over with cloves. Platters of pink meats, creamy meats, sliced wafer-thin. Whole cold fowl with legs sticking up and pink paper crowns on them. Lanterns popping into light among the trees. The gleam of white Eros against the semicircle of hedge that was turning black. Plunkety-plunk of remote Hawaiian music.

"Of course, Martin, if you must get to work, we'll start now. It's been so perfect."

"Yeh, but I'm going to break the news of you to the family pretty precious quick now, and you'll be out here often. Now, my idea for beginning my article is this. Wait, here come Aunt Em and the Herricks. Now's our chance to make our bread-and-butter speech. They've fallen for you, Orchid, just the way I knew they would. That's going to make it so much easier. I mean, their liking you before they know. Aunt Em. Judge. Mrs. Herrick.

It's been bully, and now we're catching the Mandel express back to town."

"Martin, aren't you staying for supper on the lawn? Your uncle will expect."

"Sorry, Aunt Em, but what my uncle expects, so far as I was able to gather from my interview with him just now up in the gymnasium, is that I rattle my bones over the stones between here and town in behalf of a New York paper known as *The Enquirer*."

"But, Martin, your cousins."

"They'll have to bear up, Aunt Em. Tell Celeste I'll make up that set of tennis to her next week."

"Very well, then," chimed in Mrs. Herrick, hooking her arm into Orchid's; "that's all very well for young men with tiresome things like editions to make, but I intend to keep this child here for supper. I want her to see my gardens by lantern-, by star-, and by what I hope will be moonlight, if that well-known orb behaves according to schedule."

"Mrs. Herrick!"

"Yes, why not let Miss Sargossa stay, Martin? We'll see that she gets home. Plenty will be driving in."

"Oh no, I couldn't. Martin wouldn't like me to."

"Of course she couldn't, Martin, if you

insist upon standing there with a long face about it. John Lester, don't you think he ought to want her to stay, if we want her to?"

"Get along back to town, if you must, you young scamp, you. We'll see that this little lady gets home."

"Orchid, do you want to stay?"

Did she want to stay? The pink pearl of a twilight. Mrs. Herrick with those clear friendly eyes. Did she want to stay!

"Why, Martin, not if you ——"

"Well, did you ever hear of anyone as high-handed as that nephew of yours, Mrs. Innesbrook? Of course she wants to stay."

"Yes, but you see, I came with Martin."

"Suppose you did. He's going back to town to work, as I understand it."

"Martin," said Orchid, and drew him a little aside and lifted a pair of rather wistful eyes at him over her sotto voce, "I wouldn't think of staying if you ——"

"Why, Ork, of course I want you to stay. As a matter of fact, it makes things just a bit better for me. I'll bone down to the job sooner."

"Martin, you're just saying that because you think I want to stay. Honestly, dear, if ——"

"Goosie, you, I'm saying it because I want

you to stay. Come to think about it, I not only want you to stay, but I insist that you stay. Sooner you all get to know one another, the better. Come now, no more private-conference stuff. Ladies and gentlemen, Miss Sargossa, upon advice of counsel, is going to remain. But what about getting her home? A fellow has some obligations to the girl he has out, you know."

"Don't you bother about that. There will be carful after carful driving in."

"Mind nobody vamps you."

"Martin, you silly. I won't stay late. I'll be back in town before eleven."

"Shall I call you up if I finish my article by then?"

"Don't you dare not to."

"So long, everybody. First time I ever brought a girl to a shindig and checked her there."

"Dear Martin. Dear, dear Martin."

*

Even upon an occasion as informal as supper in a garden, to starlight and lantern-light and Hawaiian music and cold hams and high plates of sandwiches and great mounds of salads, it was something of a distinction to be seated only two removes from the hostess, and that hostess Selene, with her eyes darting about for the well-being of Orchid.

"Judge Rhincoop, there's a dear, see that Miss Sargossa has some of those fresh figs. Show her how to peel them. I'm afraid she doesn't understand quite how informal our picnic spirit is."

Old man Rhincoop, full of years almost to senility but with a head like a lion and a social standing as impregnable as one, peeling fresh figs for Orchid!

"And, dear child, have you tasted those candied rose-leaves? Pass them to her, Mark. They're off my own bushes, and my chef makes them in my very own kitchen. Do nibble some. She looks as if she were made for the rôle of nibbling rose-leaves, doesn't she, Admiral Buchanan?"

"She puts them to shame. They deserve to be nibbled," said the Admiral, and cocked a wine-glass.

It was like a dream that had no awakening because you were already awake.

Afterward there was dancing to the ukuleles on a platform set up on the Innesbrook lawn.

Orchid could not dance. The young girls who were a little bitter in their patronage set up a great ado of the cooing of laughter over this. "That's a good one! What do you wager she's an ex-Follies queen? Whose little ex-Folly are you, Doris Wing? Doesn't dance. Suppose the dressmaking firm objects to the wear-and-tear on their gowns. Oh la, la, look at Allen. What do you wager they are old pals? He'd better not let Judge Herrick see him tipsy. How he ogles her. And hoity-toity, as they doubtless say it in the French room, how she will have none of him.''

But it did not matter, really. The bitter patter of the girls. The snug secure girls, like old Judge Rhincoop's granddaughters and the Wing twins.

Her little triumph. As if it mattered really to the girls who were tucked so snugly into an environment into which she only dared to venture in borrowed finery.

And so, while there was dancing, Orchid found herself with the older group that wandered off to the Herrick library. A stone vaulted room with high Gothic windows and a black-oak balcony and a stone carved fireplace that had been brought piece by piece from a palace in Ravenna. Books. Old warm fragrant bindings. Rippling row after rippling row of them. A Great Dane dog that dozed near the fender. Butlers passing silver boxes of cigars and coffee in cups in silver holders.

Mark Delano read a poem out of a priceless edition of Keats that was unlocked and lifted out of a glass case by the Judge. Lines that even Orchid had once memorized from a blackboard in the old days at the House.

> A thing of beauty is a joy for ever.
> Its loveliness increases. . . .

Orchid with her eyes on the beauty of Selene, and her heart beating to the mystery of the beauty of rhythm.

The explorer described an elephant stampede in the jungle.

A Madam Navarro sang an aria from Aïda to the accompaniment of the organ, and, later, frail things from Schubert and Lisa Lehmann.

And suddenly, all too soon, the evening was at an end. Calls for motor cars. Wraps. Missing members of family groups. For the moment, just for the moment, Orchid stood on the edge, wondering in a little panic if she were forgotten. But no, there was Mrs. Herrick standing with her forefinger against her lips and surveying the departing groups.

"Now let me see. Any of them will be glad to drive you in. Where do you live?"

"I'll drive her in, Mrs. Herrick. I'm putting up in town to-night at the club."

"You? Nonsense, Allen. You've too naughty a record for fast driving."

"Nothing of the sort. Besides, I've the limousine and chauffeur. Not even driving myself, to-night."

"I — please ——"

"I'm sure, Allen, the Dyers will be glad to tuck Miss Sargossa in with them. Where do you live, dear?"

"I know where she lives. Right on the way to my club in Gramercy Park. Glad to."

"You know where she lives? You?"

"Sure. I've been to your place, haven't I, Miss Sargossa? Do I know where you live? Well, I've occasion to. One of the liveliest little parties I ever attended took place in — Seventeenth Street, isn't it? I've reason to remember that number. Seventeenth Street, west. Am I right? Let's see: 27, isn't it?"

"Why — yes ——"

"Oh," said Mrs. Herrick. It was as if someone had lowered a shade or turned down a light. "Oh. Why, yes, of course, Allen. How good of you to see Miss Sargossa home. So nice of you to have come. Good-night."

It was exactly as if someone had lowered a shade. Or turned out a light.

*

The scalding tears. She tried to bite them back, and did, so that they lay against the surface of her eyes and stung.

Allen's was a huge fog-coloured closed car with one window just slightly opened, so that stuffiness and heat crowded in, and she asked to have it lowered more.

"Surely," said Allen, and with the car whirring and low branches lashing about them like storm, leaped up and jerked at the strap until the window fell with a clatter.

"How's that?"

"Better, thank you."

Gravel spun up against the guards. For at least ten minutes, to the lashing and the clatter, they wound out and out of the Herrick estate. And then, suddenly, the open road. Clear, swift, noiseless, and Orchid sitting straight and remote in her corner and succeeding with all her strength in forcing back the miserable impulse to cry.

At the last moment, to have a perfect day crumple like a house of cards! And Terry, young Terry, had done it.

"I think you were cruel, Mr. Terry. Just cruel, cruel, cruel. Putting things that way."

"What do you mean, 'cruel'?"

"Oh, you understand what I mean. Implying by your manner that, instead of the one dreadful party over which I had no control, there had been many. There was something deliberate about your seeming to want to place me in that light with Mrs. Herrick."

"Show me the man, if he is a man, who wouldn't want to brag about the fact he'd known you before," growled Allen, and lit a cigarette so that his face shone out in flickers. Allen was tipsy. It was difficult to judge just how tipsy except by the flare of the match. There were the same little thickening red rims under his eyes that had been there the night of the party. Heavy-looking, wet-looking red rims.

"What is the idea of the corner. To invite me to come hither?"

Ugh, he was losing no time with his tiresome parryings.

"I won't bite."

"Come, Mr. Terry, let's make the best of this ride in. Isn't Mrs. Herrick lovely?"

"There was no one on those grounds to-day lovely, except you. You're gorgeous, and you know it, and, dammit, you're as cold as an egg."

"Do, Mr. Terry, let's make this a game. Treat me the way you would any of those — those secure girls out there to-day."

"Do you think there was one on the place I would trouble to treat one way or another?"

"We're just two chance travellers going the same direction. Nice of you to give me the lift. Won't you please let it be that, sort of human-being to human-being? Not man to mannequin. Ha, how's that for a determined if not highly successful comedy effort? Don't, Mr. Terry!"

"What?"

"I — I hate being touched."

"Fire can melt ice."

"I must ask you again. Please — don't!"

"Well then, don't put thoughts into my head by snuggling off in that corner like you're afraid I'm contagious."

There might be something to that! It was politic to manage Allen Terry. Suddenly he was seeming so much tipsier than at first. In all her dreary experiences with these men who peeped so curiously into her world, there was one state she could not calmly cope with. Tipsiness. Men with lolling heads. With red threads and red rims to their eyes. There might be something to what Allen had just said. Putting the thought into his head by letting him know that she feared or detested.

"I'm sorry. It's just that it seems a little cooler in the corner. Now, is that better?"

"Dammit, you think I'm drunk, don't you?"

"Are you?"

"I don't know. I seem to be getting that way. I wasn't so very when we started. It's the opal water and old Rhincoop's bootleg gin. I don't think, though, I'm as drunk on that as I am on you. Dammit. I've been drunk on you ever since I clapped eyes on you this afternoon. Why do you think I stuck around that old ladies' frolic? Ten minutes is my limit at those neighbourhood fests, and I stayed five hours. You. You know why I'm driving in town to-night. You. Dammit. You. You. You."

It seemed wise just to grip the seat and not dare move or let him feel any of the repellant shudder.

"You're talking nonsense, Mr. Terry."

"Maybe I am, but it's great to be crazy over you. I could have murdered young Innesbrook for every moment he stuck with you. I could have knocked the head off that pie-eyed explorer and Delano and the whole pack of them every time they laid an eye on you. I could even have murdered the Judge and his wife, fussing over you the way they did. I'm mad over you, Orchid. You're made out of ice, and I'm fire to melt you."

"Don't you," she said, without moving, but her hands gripping into the upholstery; "don't you!"

"How do I know you're not egging me on?"

"I couldn't bear your touching me."

"Too fastidious, eh?"

"You're drunk."

"Drunk on you."

"You're talking nonsense."

"Maybe, but I'm seeing red with it."

"Don't!"

"Why not, Orchid? I want to be friends with you, and you tease me. You frighten me by holding me off. I've thought of you since that night, and seeing you to-day has made me realize how much I've thought of you. Since that day at the Ritz when I asked Toto to fix it for me, I've been crazy for you — crazy for you." Grinding each word of the three against her averted face with his lips.

Even then, Orchid could keep her voice low beneath her rising fear, not daring to move from him, almost as if by change of position the flame that was hovering beside her might be fanned.

"If you do that again," she said in a voice that was cool even while the scorched place where his lips had touched her burned in, "I'll call to your chauffeur to stop the car."

"You ought to be clever enough to realize that my chauffeur knows better than to obey an order like that."

Orchid *was* clever enough to know, and that was part of her rising terror. Terry must be pretty tipsy to have let his tongue run away with the saying of that.

And then Orchid, with nausea upon her and more panic than she would admit to herself, began to parry. To feed his ego.

Twenty-two miles, beside this man whose body and whose breathing she could feel, of sparring for time.

"You're not like most of the men a girl like me comes in contact with, Mr. Terry. You're rather more difficult to understand." And under her panic, to herself: Idiot. Idiot. Idiot.

"It's because so few interest me."

"The only way a girl can get very far with you is to realize from the first that you're different." (Idiot. Idiot. Idiot.)

"You said it. My governor — my family, in fact — not one of them ever really understands me. When I get my heart set on a thing nothing in God's world is going to change it. Now, do you think that I could rush around a girl like you, just to show myself a good time, the way nine out of ten of the fellows in my set do it? No. I want the girl I like to like me as much as I like her. You hear! And, dammit, I'm willing to pay for it."

The fanning breath on her face and the lips that presently, unless she could endure through it, fight through it, suffer through it, would come closer and closer.

"Don't you dare! Don't you dare, or I'll jump!"

"What?"

"Oh — nothing. I — I was just saying I — it's all in getting used to an idea."

"Look at me when you talk. I'm tired of the tip of your ear. Look around at me."

"Yes?"

"Say something to me. Call me by a love-name that will burn into me like you do. I'm drunk, all right. Yeh. I'm drunk all right, but I'm drunk on you."

"Don't! Don't. I mean, don't do it that way unless you want to spoil things. The best way to manage me, Mr. Terry, is to let me get used to an idea first."

"I'm wild for you, Orchid. Get used to that idea."

"That's because you're different from most men and don't frighten a girl in the beginning." (Idiot. Idiot. Idiot.)

MANNEQUIN

"Are you spoofing me, or are you ——"

"What do you mean?"

Miles of the talk. Miles of the talk. Miles of the futile parrying talk of holding him off. Miles and miles of the parrying. Yonkers. Spuyten Duyvil. 204th Street. 141st Street.

"Kiss me, Orchid. I'm crazy for you."

"When Toto promised me I was to meet you she said you were a difficult person to understand. Not obvious like the rest.

"I *am* different. Ask anybody who knows me. But I'm not the same man in your hands. I'm putty, I tell you. I tell you. Turn that face around: I'm crazy for it."

"Now you're talking just like every other man" (Idiot. Idiot. Idiot.) "who thinks he's talking to just another mannequin. Remember our game." Miles and miles of the parrying. 116th Street.

"I don't care how I'm talking. I'm crazy. I want to be crazy. I'll pay. Turn that face toward me. Give me that face. Dammit, I think you're trying to make a fool out of me."

"Don't — don't do that, Mr. Terry, if we're to get on!" (Martin, dear Martin, why didn't I leave with you? Martin, help me to endure this ride.) Miles and miles of the parrying. Ninty-sixth Street. Forty-ninth. Miles and miles of the parrying.

"Look here now, you beauty, you, I'm drunk enough to have the nerve, even with you. I'm going to kiss you. I'm going to kiss you, and the more you resist the more I'm going to ——"

Grinding of brakes. Blessed grinding of brakes. Curb of Seventeenth Street. Brownstone stoop. Long. Narrow. Lean. Gleam of the brave little array of the season's first geraniums in window-boxes on little iron balconies.

"How dare you do that! Take away your hand. I'm home. Let me out or I'll shout. If your chauffeur is trained not to hear, someone else will. This is my house. Let me out."

"What the — your house ——"

"Yes, you fool, you. Didn't realize that, did you? One as tipsy as you wouldn't. Let me out."

The chauffeur swinging solemnly the door. Like a dart Orchid up and out in a swirl of the fine raiment. And, strangely enough, with alertness for one so befogged, Allen out and up the steps after her.

"Look here, Orchid, you don't think I'm fool enough to let you get away with thinking I ——"

"I do. I do." The door-key slid around

so in the bottom of her bag, her frantic fingers after it. "I do. I do."

"You don't think I drove you all the way to town in order to be made a fool of like this."

"You drove me in to torture me. To humiliate me. To degrade me. No, don't you dare! I can unlock it."

"Give me, or I'll ——"

"No, I say!"

"When we get indoors I'll explain."

"When we get indoors! We're not going to get indoors. You had me intimidated during the hideous period of that long drive, but now I'm at home, and if you take one step in after me, I'll shout. Don't you dare!"

"You little devil —— " Terry with his foot in between the opened door. But Orchid, like a flash before him and with the strength born of frenzy, hurtling his shoe from between by kicking it with hers and slamming the door. Slamming the door on him standing there befuddled.

In the dim hall so full of old odours, the red glass globe with the warts in it emitting a feeble light from a newel-post, it was hard to find the keyhole of the solemn double door that led to her room. She entered it finally with the tears raining down her face. She entered it precisely as Allen Terry, dismissing his chauffeur, swung one leg over the balustrade and, stepping on to one of the little ironwork balconies of the window-boxes, walked in through the open window and took a stationary position behind one of the full-length cretonne curtains.

❋

It was not so much the reaction from the strain of that drive back to town as it was a sort of general let-down. The nerve-tearing horror of what she had been through, combined with the spectacle of herself as she stood there before her pier-glass in the borrowed finery. Tawdriness of that, and an environment that flowed up about her as murky as old water.

Nauseous reaction from a peep into a world that had seemed to fit her as closely as a silk glove. The old slit of street once more. The old odours. The pretentiousness of the borrowed finery. The eyes of Mrs. Herrick. The clear eyes of the woman who for a time had shone upon her like a sun, turning cold at the last moment. As if a shade had been drawn.

Crying a little, and yearning for just an ordinary good grin from Martin to make life something of a humorous reality again, Orchid took off her wrap, the filmy one edged in fur, fumbling a little at unfastening the shoulder-ornament, and with the fastidiousness inherent folded it, with a clinking of the released pin from its scabbard, across a chair and slid out of her dress, as slimly as a calyx stripped of petal.

It was a leisurely process, this undressing. A procedure that was a ceremonial of solemn little dainty doings. The folding-back of the couch-covers so that the sheets formed a cool envelope. The fitting of ribbon-bound trees into the slim slippers. The laying-away in their tissue and sachet of the oddments and endments of her finery. Sheer little lace things she sometimes concocted out of remnants picked up at sales.

Finally, Orchid standing before her mirror in her pink slip of the simplest of nightgowns, brushing out her hair and seeming, suddenly, someone very small and very hurt, the shimmer of the flesh glowing through her nightdress, and her neck and shoulders even more luminous.

It was then that Allen Terry, whose breathing she must have heard except for the sobby little noises in her own, stepped out and, before she could call or leap back, had his lips and his hot fumy moustache against the warmth of her shoulder.

"You cannot call out now," he said quietly, with his lips against hers, and almost as if he were druggy with her nearness. "You daren't call out now. Look how they'll find you. Here, with me. This way! I love you."

He was a vise, and she was in it, with her arms crushed up against her body so that the hair-brush dug into her from the bristle side as he tightened his embrace.

He was a vise, and he was crushing.

"Let me go," she said under a whisper, the old whisper of her childhood protection of Nana against the neighbours. "Let me go, Mr. Terry. Won't you please? Let me go. Or Mrs. Snuggs will hear and ———"

"You're beautiful."

"Listen, Mr. Terry. I'm not going to call out. I understand. You're a little dizzy from the drinks — the heat. Mr. Terry, won't you please — quietly — let me go?"

"I can't. I'm crazy for you."

"You! Let go." Suddenly, with a wrench of her body, the hair-brush clattering to the floor, she was free of him and close enough to the chair to grasp the fur-edged cape in an effort to throw it across her bare shoulders.

The gleam of her shoulders. Even in her panic Orchid was instinctively trying to blind

him to the gleam above the pink slip of gown,
by thrusting herself somehow into the filmy
wrap.

He could have had no sense of the spectacle
of himself standing there making feints after
her in every direction as she dodged back from
him.

"You maddening little devil——"

"Mr. Terry, please! Mr. Terry — please!"

All of this still under her breath, frantically
conscious of the need to keep it there, and trying breathlessly, recklessly, to throw the cape
over her shoulders. The gleam of her shoulders.

But he had her again; and this time, with
a superhuman strength which the moment
seemed to give her, when she wrenched free of
him again she left him standing a little sillily
swaying to the clinking of the ornament, and
with only the empty wrap, which he had torn
from her shoulders, in his grasp. And then
again, in the stealthy, terrible, melodramatic
fashion of one crazed with desire, he had
her in the position of being backed into a
corner.

Orchid did not want to be backed into that
corner. Orchid was afraid of being backed up
like that. Orchid was beginning to be inco-
herently, insanely afraid.

"Don't you! Don't you!"

"Elusive, maddening piece of up-staginess, you!"

"Don't you dare! You! You. Give me my cape. Give it to me, I say. You'll tear it! Please! Don't you dare — to — come — don't you dare to come ——" cried Orchid, full of a sense of the need of covering her shoulders, full of the imperative need. Afraid of his eyes and the cunning of the way he approached her. Unreservedly afraid now. Afraid of being backed into that corner.

"If you touch me —— If you ——"

"You darling!"

"Give me my cape, Mr. Terry. Give me my cape," shouted Orchid now. "Don't you dare to come nearer. I couldn't stand it. I — no — no — my cape!" And lunged out and caught at it where he held it against his chest. And as she lunged he turned away with the sheer thing gripped to him. And on that flash of his back turned to her, Orchid, wild with her fear of him, leaped!

Leaped upon him with the force of her body; so with the force of her frenzy that Terry, befuddled young Terry, tripped and fell forward upon his face. So that on that instant, a triumphant frenzied instant of seeing red, Orchid was literally astride him, battering against his

back with her fists, pummelling him between
the sobs of hysteria.

"You drunken wretch. You wretch. How
dare you. How dare you!" Pummelling and
pummelling him with her two futile hands,
and unstrung now to the point of laughing
through the tears.

And, strangely enough, when Terry in his
befuddlement pitched forward from the sudden-
ness of Orchid's leap at his back, he did so with
a cry. A long thin gurgle of a cry that stuck in
the air as if a knife had been hurled. And then,
in a feeble sort of way, he fought back, breathing down with little gurgles into the chiffon
wrap as he clutched it, and somehow struggling. Struggling against the feeble pummel-
lings of Orchid. And suddenly, with another
gurgle into the chiffon wrap, he lay there
limp, letting her pummel.

"You! You! I want you to get up. I want
you to get out of here. I want you never to
let me see your horrid, your drunken, your
degenerate face again. If you do — you hear
me — I'll tell the man I'm going to marry.
A man in your own social class. And unless
you get up and get out of here quietly, without
my landlady or anyone seeing you, I'm going
to tell him. You hear me. My fiancé. And
he'll kill you, only killing is too good for you.

You get out! You get out. Get out, you.
Get up and get out."

Orchid sitting there on her knees beside him,
beating and pummelling him with her frail
fists, and the tears lashing, and her mouth
twisted into a rhomboid into which ran the
tears. Her face blanched. Her face twisted.

And strangely, and to her growing terror, he
did not get up. It was as if she could feel,
rather than see, the faint creep of limpness pass
over his body.

"Mr. Terry," she cried, poking his shoulder
with a gingerly held finger, "Mr. Terry."
And then rolled him over, against no resist-
ance, to the spectacle of a stark, stiff-looking
face. To a stiff face with the eyes and mouth
open. To a stiff face. . . .

"Mr. Terry!"

There was something that moved, though.
Something widening and widening on the pink
chiffon cape as he held it clutched to his bosom.
Something widening. Something wet. Something sticky!

"Mr. Terry," cried Orchid, this time on a
little shriek, and reached over with rigid fingers to lift the cloak. It came partially off in a
little cloud of pink, but then it resisted.

With the garment clutched to his heart
as he had jerked it away from her, Terry had

plunged forward on to the dagger. The rose-quartz-and-filigree dagger of the unsheathed ornament.

The cape would not lift. It was pinned there in the widening stain to the heart of Allen Terry. Pinned to the dead, the punctured heart of Allen Terry. Pinned there by the jewelled sword.

To her it might have been moments, it might have been days, but actually it was one hour and fifteen minutes that Orchid sat there on her knees beside the stiff upturned face of Allen Terry, with the eyes that were so terribly wide open.

Just sat with her hands laid out like shells on her lap, and the silence of her face like her silence carved into the face of a graven image.

Tick-tock, went a clock on her dresser, as if every second were sucking her in on the tick and ejecting her on the tock. Tick. Tock.

The stain had stopped widening, and, grotesquely, that made the silence seem bigger. That stain, stabbed there to the heart of Allen Terry.

After a while, as remotely as if from another world, the telephone under its cretonne doll began to ring; and on that sound, seated there crouched, Orchid began to laugh, and, laugh-

ing, dragged herself over on her knees to answer
it.

"Yes?" Her own voice was such a squeak!
It was to laugh. A dried little squeak. No,
it was like a little dried pea, rolling around in
a little dry pod. "Yes?"

"Hello, darling. What's the comedy? Home
all right? O my gosh, but I've been kicking
myself ever since for not asserting my he-
man rights and bringing you home with me.
Orchid, you there?"

"Yes. Yes." Oh, oh, that little dried-pea-
in-a-pod of a voice.

"Sweetheart, guess what? I beat the deadline by an hour. I'm down at Park Row.
Frightfully hot booth. Morning edition just
off the press with my full-page spread in it.
Would your scorpion of a landlady mind, do
you think, if I drop around with it? I'll ring
two longs and a short and you open the door.
It's only eleven-thirty. I want you to see it
set up in print before you go to bed. It looks a
bit sensational, coloured illustrations and all,
but it will make a dent. You were a darling
to-day, Ork. Who brought you in? Felt un-
easy, hang it. Listen, darling, you there?"

"Yes. Yes." Dried little pea rolling around
in its pod. Couldn't help laughing. Couldn't
help laughing.

"Don't mind, do you, if I pop around? Won't come in. Just hand you the paper. Orchid, you there?"

Little dried pea in its pod. Wouldn't even rattle its "yes." Couldn't. Suddenly, Orchid in a limp heap on the floor beside the telephone doll.

"Hang this telephone. What the dickens? What fell? Did you drop the receiver, Orchid? Hello, central. Am I still connected? Well, the receiver may be off the hook, but there's a balled-up connection somewhere. Blamed telephone service. Hello, Orchid, that you? Hello, hello, hello. Funny — darn funny —— "

It was seventeen minutes before twelve when Martin hopped out of a taxicab without dismissing it, and, bulk of Sunday morning edition of the *Enquirer* under his arm, ran a little worriedly up the steps of the brown-stone house in Seventeenth Street.

There was a gleam of light through a rift between the cretonne curtains. Two rings and a short. And then two deeper and longer rings and a short.

Silly to feel worried, but what the deuce ——

After a while, just as he was ready to plunge a nervous and insistent finger into the button, the door was opened by Mrs. Snuggs herself,

in curl-papers and the blue cotton wrapper with
the three sateen ruffles.

"Mrs. Snuggs, I'm sorry. Most awfully
sorry. But I was talking to Miss Sargossa just
now over the telephone and suddenly she was
cut off in a most curious fashion. Central insisted we were still connected. Just went off
the wire as if she had fallen. Thought I'd
jump into a taxi and come around. Might have
fainted or got ill or something. She didn't
hang up. Don't mind knocking, do you, and
handing her this newspaper with my compli-
ments?"

Mrs. Snuggs did mind.

"She's home all right. Seems to me I've
heard commotion enough in there this evening.
Step in a minute, and I'll knock. Hate goings-
on." Mrs. Snuggs standing there in the black
hall with the nub of red gaslight burning into
it, rapping her bony fingers against the door
and inclining a spiky curl-papered head.

"Seems to be nobody there now."

"But there is, Mrs. Snuggs; I just spoke to
her."

"Funny. Ve-ry funny."

"Here, let me. I'll rattle the knob. She
may have dozed off. Water may be running.
Orchid, hey. Say, it's me. Martin. Martin
and Mrs. Snuggs. Never mind opening the door

if you're not dressed or something. I've just brought you the morning edition. Thought you might want to look it over. I'll leave it right here next to the door and hop along. Must have been cut off. Orchid! I say, Orchid?"

Suddenly Martin turned to Mrs. Snuggs, his horn-rimmed glasses burning into the gloom.

"We've got to force in, Mrs. Snuggs," he said. "Something is wrong."

*

Even after the noises began, and the tele-phonings, and the hurrying of feet, and the nerve-splitting hysterics of Mrs. Snuggs, and the pop-eyed peering-in of neighbours and lodgers, and Orchid lying there in her long swoon beside the telephone doll, and Allen with his face up and the chiffon wrap pinned to his heart, one thought in the daze and the pain kept racing around the inside of Martin's head like a rat in its cage.

That wasn't really Orchid lying there in that huddle. Presently Terry, who was drunk, would get up and brush himself off. Terry hadn't been stabbed. What the devil was that howling hyena of a landlady letting the crowds into the room for?

And, worst of all, there was the one thought

that kept racing around so, making it seem as if he had two heads, both of them aching.

The Sunday morning edition there at his feet, open, ironically enough, as someone had kicked it in passing, to the first of his series of feature articles. It was devilish that here was the first of them staring at him in print, and Monday's and Tuesday's follow-up stories already set up, beyond recall.

It was more devilish and it was more ironical that now, standing there with his two head-aches in the daze of the coming of the coroners, the paper should lie open, there at his feet, to his article:

SEXLESS JUSTICE
GIVE THE WOMAN MURDERER HER CHANCE TO ATONE FOR HER CRIME

Hang it all, a fellow just couldn't think. That howling hyena of a landlady! What made Orchid stay in the swoon? It was too silly. Life had just toppled, that was all, carrying him down under the débris.

What the dickens made Orchid stay in that swoon? She must come up to explain. That red-faced fellow with the limp. Seen him before somewhere. Sure enough! District captain from the old days when Martin was police reporter down in Seventh precinct. Captain Gallagher. Well, well, what was all the row about? Why were they letting in that string of people? Why the blazes was everybody writing in notebooks? Measuring. Just like the old police-reporting days.

"Hello, Cap. What are you doing here?"

"Hi, Innesbrook? Haven't seen you in a coon's age. Busted out of police reporting into big time, eh? Looks ugly, don't it?"

"What?"

"She stabbed him, sure as fate."

"Who?"

"Martin," cried Orchid, and opened her eyes and reached out her hand. "Martin, I dreamed — he — he — fell forward. On the ornament — stabbed!"

"Sure he did. Yeh. We found him that way. Laying face up with the dagger plunged in. Looks like he fell on it, don't it? Don't say anything more, little lady. Put your foot in it every time you open your mouth. Just sit there quietly. We're getting around to you."

"Didn't you hear?" shouted Martin. "Didn't you hear? He fell on it!"

"Yah, I heard," said Captain Gallagher. "Here, you, Steve, make a diagram of the position of that body. No, chalk it around on the carpet."

"He fell on his face," Martin could hear himself shouting to himself, but trying to stand calmly by with his hand on Orchid's.

"Martin, am I crazy? What has happened? Martin, I didn't do it. I didn't ——"

"I know you didn't," Martin kept saying, standing there patting her, "I know you didn't." And then to himself, through the yelling noises in his head: I know she didn't do it, and what's more I don't care if she did. And — what's — more — I — don't — care — if — she — did. No matter. No matter. She's mine, through thick and thin. Through thick she's mine, and thin.

But the frenzy of the idea that was chasing around like a captive rat in his brain was unbearable to him.

He wanted to rush out somewhere, anywhere, everywhere, to gather in — to gather in to himself somehow the morning edition of the Sunday *Enquirer*. Destroy it! The morning edition of the *Enquirer*, already released in hundreds of thousands, and carrying, each number of them, the headline in flame:

SEXLESS JUSTICE
GIVE THE WOMAN MURDERER
HER CHANCE TO ATONE FOR
HER CRIME

BOOK III

BOOK III

ONE thing about horror after you were drenched with it, there came a certain stage beyond which your capacity to feel seemed to cease. You became numb.

Orchid was grateful for the numbness. It always seemed to her, sitting there in the incredible confinement of a cell, that if she were to stick pins into her wrists she would be absolutely impervious to a sense of pain.

Incredible confinement in a cell. Why, one only read of people in cells. It was something associated with newspaper headlines and political history. There was a picture of Oscar Wilde seated in his cell with his head in his hands, that used to hang in the show-window of a Fifth Avenue art dealer. But that, after all, was on the remote and impersonal plane. Even down in Prince Street among the riff-raff, the fathers of playmates had got into difficulties and been thrown into jail. But never so that you could realize it in terms of cells. Just the talk and the prattle in the free out-of-doors about these fathers in jails. And never, that Orchid could remember, had there been a mother in jail.

Being in one herself now, with its granitoid floor and its cot and basin and bucket, was absolutely beyond the mere perceptions. Most of the time one was just insensate with horror. Orchid sat, sometimes, dully wondering whether, if pins were plunged into her, they would have drawn pain or blood. And the days stalked by. One by one by one. So many wooden soldiers, stalking.

Occasionally people came in. To the clanking of keys. Always to the clanking of keys. Wardens admitting them into the cell with a clanking of keys. The beat of the clanking of keys in her brain. The maddening beat of keys clanking; and the people were wooden soldiers. The wooden soldier of Martin, with his face the colour of the granitoid floor, trying to get her to talk.

And there was never anything to say. Sometimes, at his eagerness and the nearness of his face peering at her through the incredibility of iron bars between them, something strange and cold and angry rose in Orchid. Against Martin. Those stripes down his face, why, those stripes were bars, between them.

He was part of the system. He lived in that world out there. Part of the system. The mysteriousness. The vast granitoid-coloured system that had her caught there, behind bars, while the days marched by like soldiers. The immutable wooden soldiers. To the clanking of the keys. Clank, clank, to the clanking of the keys.

There was someone else who tried to make her talk, with the same desperate kind of eagerness as Martin's, and he was a wooden soldier too. The wooden soldier of a lawyer. Wilder Deneen. He was getting something ready. Preparing the case. Dully, with the rim of her fagged brain, Orchid knew that. Knew it through the noxious smells of iodoform and roach disinfectant and prison corridors. One night the creature who shared the adjoining cell to hers had been led frothing at the mouth through those corridors. The tramping of feet being led somewhere, and the clanking of keys. The clanking, the clanking of keys.

It was useless trying to talk. The keys hurt so as they clanked into one's brain. And there was nothing to say.

That seemed the dreariest part. There was nothing to say.

If only Martin would not keep coming and pleading and begging and pressing his face against the stripes that were between her and him. Coming and coming. And begging to be forgiven. For what? Dear Martin. Articles?

Oh yes, of course. Dear old Mart, it was hard trying to feel enough even to smile at him. What did they matter? What did anything matter? If only he wouldn't keep stewing so much about the articles. Nobody read them anyhow. And if they did — as if anything mattered that much! As if anything could ever matter again.

It was useless trying to talk.

There was nothing to say.

*

Nor were the days of the actual trial so very different from the weeks of the days of the wooden soldiers and the clanking of the keys.

The clanking of the keys. The days still moved to the rhythm of them. The clanking of the keys.

Except that now, to Orchid, the days were no longer wooden soldiers. Each one was a sea of the bloated faces.

Bloated faces, pressing against the window-panes from the outside of the courtroom. Bloated faces. Along the benches. Against walls. And policemen brandishing clubs to keep more of them from storming in. And the sea kept lapping slightly within its basin of courtroom, day after day, swaying with its bloated faces. The sea of the courtroom of the bloated faces.

The first day of the trial it had almost seemed that she must drown in that sea. Drown in the gaze of all the greedy eyes sliding over her, and the lips of the women, wet from running their tongues over them, and the beating Adam's apples of the men.

One dared not faint. What if they should punish one for fainting at one's own trial? And yet, terror of that thought, what if one could not help fainting?

It helped to sit knotted tightly, and after the first several days even the horror of looking out over the sea of the bloated faces became anæsthetized. It became like the nights, when, trying to sleep, half the time she was dimly battling her way through the sea of the faces. And always to the clanking of the keys. The clanking of the keys that never, never ceased in her brain.

Sometimes everything in the courtroom revolved. The faces pressing in from the outside. The policemen brandishing the clubs. The reporters focusing their cameras. The running hither and thither of the stenographers and clerks.

Finally, and austerely, the entrance of the Judge in his robes, and the rising of the courtroom, and the falling of the gavel. Everything revolving.

Why, that was Judge Herrick!

*

There was a garden, yes, there was a garden somewhere — and here was the Judge, and out there in the garden, that garden somewhere, was Selene Herrick.

Why, no! There were the eyes of Selene Herrick out in the sea of the bloated faces. Day after day. Third row left. Aisle. There was a garden; and yet, every day, here, in the sea of the bloated faces, the eyes of Selene Herrick. The white marcelled hair of Selene Herrick. The eyes of Selene Herrick were light-houses in the fog of the bloated sea.

Day after day of the dim, the remote, the un-real procedure of the drama of the courtroom milling around the nucleus of the prisoner's chair. And the prisoner was Orchid. And there in the third row left were the eyes of Selene, into which she could look. Into which she could flee. Into which she could, silently, and without the flicker of white passiveness of face, sob.

*

The selection of the jury, panelling, they called it, was a procedure that Orchid, with

[246]

her poor rag of interest in things, watched in a detached impersonal manner.

The jurymen sat in a pen. There was one who was like a tomato: a wide, over-ripe, fat little tomato. And the long lean one was a plumber, and his name was Slatt.

If only the clicking of the cameras and the craning of the necks and the comings and the goings would not keep jerking her back to the consciousness, however numb, that the picking of the jury was the picking of the men who were to determine everything.

Why, that must be why Martin's face, out there in the sea, every minute of every day was all full of little wrinkles, as if his anxiety were crawling over his face.

As if it mattered. Dear Martin, out there. I don't matter enough to bring one single line to your face. Your dear far-away face.

Jurymen. There was one named Anderson up before the judge, and there was something he would not believe in. Capital punishment. No, he was not to be a juryman. They were sending him away, and he had seemed a kind man. There was another. The foreman, with a long drooping moustache that made him look like a .walrus. His name was Fudge. Herman Fudge. It made the courtroom laugh. Oh Fudge. Oh Fudge. How drearily she could laugh, too, repeating it along with the court-room. Oh Fudge. Gavel. Gavel. Oh Fudge, dear Martin, I'm not worth the crawling lines. Oh Fudge, dear woman out there with the two lighthouses for eyes, to think that you should care! And to think that I care so terribly that you should care, when really — really — nothing matters.

*

All day long the jury sat in its stall looking as if it had no legs. Twelve of them from the waist up. Every morning at half after eleven the walrus had a glass of milk brought him, into which he dropped two tablets; and, when he had drunk, sucked in the ends of his moustache and wiped them two ways with his handkerchief, and then gave a stroke to each eyebrow as if they too were wet with milk. The walrus was in the fountain-pen business, and at the end of the trial presented each of his jury with a fountain-pen in a box, medicine-dropper and all. There was a round, red-haired juryman named Baker who defied his name by being a butcher. He was the tomato. And another was named Duvonnie, a building contractor. And there were Sewell and Mix and Longini. Orchid could recite them all, down to the twelfth one, named Gwirt. He had a chin, but appeared not to have. It was part of the fantasy of the dream, being able to sit there counting her jurymen. Naming them. Nick-naming them. It kept her from feeling the madness.

The terribleness of the district attorney. The terribleness of that man. Now cunning, with his eyes wizened up. Now glowering. Now thundering. Now mimicking. Now shouting. Now bellowing. Now making hissing, whispering sounds.

When the time comes for me to go upon that witness chair, don't let him bellow at me, God, please, God.

The bellowing. The cunning. The concentrated terribleness of the district attorney. His harping! His harping upon a scene which was branded in fire into her memory.

If only, oh God, oh God, why did you let me. If only I had not turned his face up! That's why they think I did it. That makes it seem that the dagger was plunged in. Wanton cruel murder. The district attorney kept saying and saying and saying that. The clankings of the keys in her brain were to the beat and the tempo of the district attorney saying and saying that. But I tell you he fell on it. I tell you he fell forward on it. The shouting in her brain. The silent shouting of that, all through the days; and then the strange incongruous anger against Martin. Out there. Part of the scheme. God, won't you help them to see that Mr. Terry fell face forward on to it? That was his name. To think that someone just named Mr. Terry should have caused all this. God, won't you help them to understand that he fell on it?

What if I should fall all to little pieces when the district attorney begins to make the mouths at me and to yell at me and to make claws of his fingers at me? Don't let him, God. Don't let him yell at me and make my brain fall to pieces.

The Deneen wooden soldier, with the bulging brief-case, was kind. If only, though, he wouldn't keep coaching. What to say and when to say it. Like a rehearsal for a play. A tragedy, or was it a comedy? As if there was anything to say, except to tell it all simply and as it happened. Except for the shame. Oh, the shame of the ride into town. How to tell that? Orchid, with the poor numbed edge of her brain, could never bring herself to face, even in rehearsal, the sea of the bloated faces with such a tale. The tale of that ride into town. The pink nightdress and the cloak with which she sought to cover it. The dagger which, clutching to himself, Terry had pitched and fallen on to. If only she had not rolled him over. That dagger sticking straight up!

The witnesses were full of the importance of that. The district attorney, and the doctors, too. Mr. Terry lying straight up with the cloak pinned to him. O God, make them understand I didn't know. *He* didn't even know. He fell on it — accident —— O God, won't you please ——

What if, when they get me on the stand, those eyes, her eyes out there, the Lighthouses, should desert me? O Martin, with all those worry-lines crawling over your face, don't let her desert me. God. Don't let Martin desert me, God. Don't let the Judge. If only the Judge would look at me.

It was true, the Judge did not, except to let his eyes pass lightly over her with the thin frigidity of ice. They were neutral eyes. They were the stern eyes of one who might have been computing to the feather's weight the balance of a pair of scales. Scales of Justice. It was as if the eyes of the Judge Herrick that Orchid remembered, back there, in a garden, in another eternity, it was as if those friendly eyes had turned to pebbles.

"Martin, why won't the Judge look at me?" she asked one day through the bars.

Poor Martin, he answered her with one of the sobbing kind of slip-ups that tripped his speech constantly these days.

"It must be because public opinion, Orchid, in this case, is at a peculiarly high pitch. All this justice talk that's abroad. As if it is not sufficient that he has the reputation for being the most fair-minded Judge on the bench of this state, he has made a ball-bearing machine out of his mind in this case, to weigh the evidence. To weigh. To weigh. The public is on guard for sexless justice and all such, and I guess I've done my bit to make it that way. Orchid, Orchid, will you ever forgive me?"

There he was again at the will-you-ever-forgive-me.

"Of course it won't matter in the end. Everybody knows you'll be acquitted and exonerated. But now I think I understand how the Greek prisoners used to feel when they made them build their own pyres under them. I've thought of it so often. That's what I've done."

As if it mattered.

"Every day since this trial has been on, the district attorney has scored one point after another quoting from those cursed articles of mine."

As if it mattered.

"And every time he scores, I want the earth to open up and swallow me and the articles together."

MANNEQUIN

Those articles again. Those articles again. If only Martin would cease haranguing about them and worrying the lines deeper into his face.

"Orchid, don't worry, dear. I beg that of you. Let the district attorney have his day. He's the sort that always rides in big in the early part of a trial. Dearest, if only you would come out of your apathy. Deneen knows just when to crash in with his big facts. I won't be able to amount to much as a witness, unless I can get in some quick licks. The district attorney will see to that. But there is a way out. Only, dearest, you must help more. I don't ask you to play to the grandstand; you know that, dearest. Only come to life. Come out of your coma. Let the jury see you in the warm flesh and blood. What the papers describe as your 'icy indifference' has been against you up to now, Orchid. They are not wise enough to know that you are frozen with horror. That's what Deneen means when he keeps trying to snap you out of your apathy. Orchid, dearest, won't you, can't you, thaw a little? For my sake?"

"Martin, I would, dearest, you know that! I would. Only, isn't it curious? Isn't it terrible? I can't feel anything. I can't realize anything, Martin, except that somehow, some way, I am going to wake up and find it a dream."

"Orchid, dearest, can't you even if it — if it's a matter of life and death?"

"Life — and — death?"

"I don't mean that! But can't you think that it is? Mightn't it help to look at it that way? Let them know about you, dearest, the things I know. The things Deneen knows. Show your jury that you are innocent."

"I'll try, Martin, I'll try."

"Bear in mind, Orchid, that they want to know every little thing about you. Bear that in mind as you sit there before them. Make them realize your inability to have done the — that thing. Keep looking at me, darling, for reminder. Doesn't it help you to see me out there?"

"Yes. Yes. And Mrs. Herrick. Martin, does she think I ——"

"Don't let her think. Everybody is talking about the fact that she hasn't missed a single session. They even say she and the Judge had a row on the subject. He doesn't want her to sit in on his cases. Most judges don't want family around. She never has before, but ——"

"Do you think, Martin, she thinks —— I couldn't stand that."

"Then convince Mrs. Herrick of your innocence, Orchid! Show her and your jury the sweet, adorable side. Show them how utterly incapable you are of any of the allegations. It would help, Orchid, dearest, if you would."

"I'll try, Martin. I couldn't bear it, somehow, if she didn't know ——"

*

If the Judge and his wife had not exactly quarrelled, they had closely approached it.

Curious and sudden perversity of Selene. In the one case in which he most wanted himself free to marshal his unfettered forces, she, who had so unswervingly aided and abetted him, now suddenly stood alien.

More than that, her unprecedented insistence upon being present at his court was not only upsetting, but frightening.

It reminded the Judge of the strange perverse Selene of those years after the loss of their child, when she had inhabited the borderless regions of nervous breakdown. When she had lived for six months in a sanatorium. When she had been a stranger to him. When for hours at a time she had sat brooding in enormous silence. When she had taken on convictions that, more often than not, were vagaries.

There was something alarmingly reminiscent

of the poor lustreless Selene of those years of nervous breakdown and yearnings and self-reproaches.

Never, though, in the time since her recovery, had Selene even once desired, much less dared, to break in upon the unwritten laws of their household.

No favours or dispensations to be asked in behalf of this or that potential voter, seeking office of one sort or another.

No member of the family ever to visit the courtroom while the Judge was presiding.

No member of the family even to question the Judge upon the outcome of some important trial of his in session, or to break in upon his period of evening retreat to his study during the process of such trial.

Those were some of the unwritten but inviolable tenets of the Herrick household.

Evening after evening, during the procedure of a trial of importance, it was nothing unusual for the Judge to disappear from the dinner-table, to be seen no more until breakfast, or even to have dinner carried in to his desk.

And Selene guarded him. And now, here in a case not only of notorious and spectacular importance in itself, but, because of a peculiar tension of aroused public psychology, one which demanded every ounce of his unfettered resources, here was the old, the alien, the remote Selene of the unhappy days following their loss. The old unreasonable Selene.

Night after night of the nervous tension of her presence, added to the more than sufficient nervous tension of this nation-arresting case, outside his study door. Scraping against it occasionally like a little dog craving admission. Begging just the opportunity to sit beside him while he worked, the chance to question him. The hope in her that somehow, in some way, a word might be dropped about the case. A word about the prisoner.

Her morbid interest. Her morbid obsession, rather, just because of what had been her first-hand meeting with the Sargossa girl.

It was not like the Selene of these later years to lose her control again this way. And all apparently just because of the brief personal contact with the prisoner. It was upsetting, of course, having it happen as it did. The Judge tried to bear all that in mind. Women could be like that. Supersensitive. As a matter of fact, it was enough to get on anyone's nerves, having two young people leave a garden party to crash into tragedy, when that garden party happened to be yours!

But not to the point of creating in Selene an insanity, an absorption without rhyme or reason. Or of causing between them the first high words in more than seventeen years.

Selene daring to insist upon sitting in his court. Chattering to him in terms of freedom of the will. The old wranglings between them that had marked those first few years of adjustment in their married life. Freedom of will. Courts open to the public. Madness.

"Selene, this is outrageous. I am ashamed of you."

"I want to sit in on this case, John Lester. You cannot forbid me the freedom of the court any more than you can any other American citizen."

"You are talking like a mad woman."

"Maybe I am, a little."

"Well then, it is a difficult and responsible time for you to upset my nerves as well. If you are so concerned over the outcome of this case, you had better see to it that my mind is kept clear and my nerves unharassed."

"John, John, I want to do that. Terribly. Only there are some things about this case, John, that I — I seem to know with my heart. If you would only let me talk.

"I will not have opinions."

"But, John, this ——"

"If you make it necessary, Selene, I'll take a room in a hotel or go to a club and not come home at all during the period of this trial."

"I won't, John. I'm sorry. I have nothing to say, then. I promise. Only, John, if you love me, if you feel sorry for me, John, if you want to save me from becoming the — the old way — I — John, I promise — not a word to you throughout the period of the trial — only let me sit in at the sessions, dear. That isn't asking much, John. I am needed there. I mean I just want to sit there, quietly. Like anyone else in court. Just quietly, John. And never a word to you evenings. One way or another. I know, dear. I know the eye of the public is upon you as never before. I know how much depends upon your keeping your mind clear and open. And you will keep it more open this time than ever, John, won't you, dear? Won't you? I promise you, John. Not a word to you, ever. Only let me sit in at the sessions. If you love me, if you pity me, John, let me come to the sessions."

The spectacle of her there on her knees with her arms about his knees and her tear-lashed face up to his, made him afraid for her.

"John, if you don't, if you don't let me, I can't bear it. I won't bear it. I want to sit in; I have to sit in on those sessions."

He was afraid for her.

"All right, dear. All right. Sh-h-h, nothing to cry about. All right."

*

Why, there were Toto and Cyd and Denise and Clarice and Mr. Mandel and Myrrh. One by one in the witness chair. Usually only for an instant. A "yes." A "no." An "I don't know." An "I never saw her until she came to work at Drecotte's." "To the best of my knowledge, sir." "Thank you, that will be all." "No, sir." "Yes, sir." "No, your Honour." "Yes, your Honour."

All except Toto. Toto seemed to have more to say. Toto seemed wanting to help.

And the district attorney didn't want her to help.

"You say you introduced her to the deceased?"

"Yes, one day at the Ambassador Show he says to me, he says ——"

"Yes or no."

"Yes — sir ——"

"Were you present at the party given at the home of the defendant on the evening of April second?"

"You see, it was thisaway. My friend, he says to me, he says ——"

"Yes or no?"

"Well, he don't need to holler at me like that, Your Honour, does he?"

"Answer all questions put to you, Miss, in the most direct manner possible."

"Yeh, your Honour. Well, yes, I was present. You see, it was thisaway ——"

"Was the defendant your hostess that evening?"

"Yes, you see ——"

"Were there drinks?"

"Yeh, but ——"

"At what hour did this party break up?"

"I — don't remember ——"

"Four o'clock in the morning?"

"No, it wasn't more than ——"

"Three?"

"N-no."

"Two?"

"Maybe. But look here, there are some things I want to tell him about, Your Honour, that I can't get said with just a 'yes' or a 'no.' Orchid didn't want ——"

"Answer to the point. Was the murdered man ——"

"Your Honour, I object."

"Objection sustained."

"Was the late Mr. Terry very marked in his attentions to Miss Sargossa?"

"Your Honour, I object."

"Objection sustained."

"That will be all. Next."

It was too incredible. All this. I must thaw. I must thaw. For Martin, for her, for the jury. For the Walrus, the Tomato, and the Slatt. Suddenly, now, clouds were coming up on every side. The girls. What they said in just the "yes" and the "no" made it seem so different. The curling of the district attorney's face. Why, Myrrh had just sat stiffly, as if hypnotized, answering without taking her eyes from his. And once she said "yes" when she meant "no," and tried to get it back. It was an important "No." Important for Orchid, sitting there with her nails in her palm. But he would not let the "yes" be unsaid. How he barked. How he meowed. How he twisted his face, to frighten. Poor little Clarice, she had looked so bold and painted to the jury, but she had wanted to cry, of pity and of fright. Orchid could tell, the way the flanges of her nose quivered. The district attorney barking so, and all of them, bold, painted, naughty-looking girls wanting to help, and yet, by very token of their gaudy and naughty appearances, impeding things. Clouds were coming up. Ah, there was Martin. Now, now, dear Martin, you tell them. Why weren't they letting Martin talk?

"Object!"

"Objection sustained."

"Object!"

"Objection sustained."

Why, they were not letting Martin talk at all. Just the yes's and the no's. Poor Martin, in his worry, tossing himself about so in the witness chair and throwing out a gesture only to be caught up, held there, silenced there.

"Object!"

"Objection sustained."

"Object."

"Objection sustained."

Never mind, dear. As if it really mattered. Only there were so many things, so many things that Martin could tell them. Martin, sh-h-h, you mustn't! Contempt of court. Martin!

"But I say, your Honour, am I not to be given the opportunity to explain that unless certain conditions are taken into account, this case, because of circumstances that involve my behaviour and my writings, may become a pernicious example of baiting the woman?"

"Order!"

"But, your Honour, public hysteria may swing too far. It is conceivable that this jury may be afraid *not* to convict this woman ——"

[263]

MANNEQUIN

"This court is called to order! Your re-marks are out of order, sir!"

"But, your Honour ——"

"Next! Mrs. Emanie Snuggs."

Why, there was Mrs. Snuggs. Poor dear Martin, how pastily, frighteningly white he was, climbing down from the witness chair to make way for Mrs. Snuggs.

Yes, there was Mrs. Snuggs. All in black, looking like an embalmed lady who had suddenly risen to take part in the wake. Mrs. Emanie Snuggs. Now who could have named her Emanie? And who could have rigged her up like a funeral? Her daughter-in-law, no doubt, who did light housekeeping in the first-floor back. Yes, those fawn-coloured slippers with the black patent-leather stripes, like a zebra, belonged to the daughter-in-law. They used to dry of their cleaning-fluid on the window-sill. They must wear the same size, Mrs. Snuggs and her daughter-in-law. Now, what was Mrs. Snuggs to talk about? Why, about you, of course. What was Mrs. Snuggs going to say? And why was Martin looking all white again, and in that terrible, that pulled way of a lace curtain on a stretcher? Dear Martin, he had done his best, wanting to testify. Only Deneen and the district attorney, they fought so. And the objections, the objections sustained and overruled. Words. And just "yes," just "no." Why? Why? And now here was Mrs. Snuggs. They were letting Mrs. Snuggs talk.

"Indade, sir, not to be wanting to answer except whin I'm spoken to, thim was goings-on. For a woman trying to run a reshpectable house, thim was ——"

"At what time did you first notice high words and disturbances in the room of the defendant?"

"It's hard to say, sir, as to the time o' night they got goin' on that party of April second. I was a-sittin' over a midnight cup of tay in my sitting-room, sir — I'm a great one for my cup of tay before retiring — and all of a sudden over my head, like to split it, like there was jumpin' divils, I ——"

"Could you identify the voice of the defendant?"

"I could that, sir."

"Were any of the lodgers or neighbours disturbed by the sounds from the room of the defendant on the night of the party in question?"

"There was complaints comin' in to me all of the nixt day, and a crowd a-gathering that night out on the sidewalk."

"Then what happened?"

"Bein' a self-reshpectin' woman, known for runnin' a reshpectable house, I ——"

"To the point, Madam. Then what happened?"

"I wint up whin the noises got deefening and knocked on the door."

"Did the defendant open it?"

"No, sir, nobody opened it, the noise being that deefening."

"Then what did you do?"

"I opens the door and I walks in."

"What did you see?"

"Such goings-on. I'm too reshpectable a woman to ——"

"Did you see the defendant?"

"The who?"

"Miss Sargossa."

"I did that!"

"What was she doing?"

"She was a-sitting in Mr. Terry's lap, God rest his soul, and ——"

"And what? And what? Proceed, my good woman."

"And he was a-rocking her like a baby and ——"

"Don't be afraid. Proceed, my good woman."

"And she was clapping her hands and playing paddy-cake ag'inst his chist."

[266]

"That will do. Next!"

"Oh. Oh. Oh. Oh, Mrs. Snuggs!" Orchid, before she could control it, crying out. Shouting out!

Gavel. Gavel. "Order in the Court!"

But it was terrible. Her tongue was all swollen like a dry hot potato. To sit there, a prisoner, in the maze of the lies. And, as if the stretched face of Martin and the Lighthouse eyes of Mrs. Herrick did not make it unbearable enough, there were the bloated faces of the sea. Sniggering out there. But it was terrible. There must be a way not to hear any more. It was as if she were a hunted thing, looking here, looking there. Twisting her handkerchief. Letting her eyes dart along the double row of the jury-box. The Walrus, the Tomato, and the Slatt. The immobile jury-box. The craning-forward jury-box. The high windows with figures perched on the sills. Patches of sky. City sky. Grey sky. Impersonal sky. The Judge in his robes in the box. The fair, square Judge, who would not look at her. The fair, square, harassed-looking Judge. Somehow he looked so much older, so much more tired, so much more haggard. It was terrible. The whanging of the witnesses, and Orchid shutting out the sound of it by a trick of tensing her ear-drums so that all she heard was a rushing as of water — a rushing as of water.

There were two doctors. One of them looked like Shakespeare and the other like a potato on two toothpicks. They kept talking and drawing with their fingers in the air, and — no — no — there was the ornament! The rose-quartz-and-filigree gilt thing. Take it away! The jury passing it from man to man. Something was closing down. Allen Terry must have been stabbed, the doctors were saying, lying face up, dagger plunged in. Mr. Terry must have been stabbed. Martin's face was all pulled by the curtain-stretcher into just a smear, and the eyes that had been lighthouses were going out. Mr. Terry had been stabbed. "Mr. Terry, if you please, had not been stabbed!" cried Orchid, rising and striking out with both arms as if to ward off a blow. "Mr. Terry had not been stabbed! You see," she cried, "it was this way — " rising, and swooning as she rose.

The rushing as of water ——.

*

It was the day. To Wilder Deneen it was as if, for the fifteen days preceding it, he had been talking against the granite side of the image with silence carved into its face.

Orchid felt it, too, wanting so desperately all the while to care enough to heed and to profit. But the sense of being locked in granite that would not let her out.

They wanted her to wear the black dress with the white organdie collar. All right. But as if it mattered. There were newspaper photographs of her, it seemed, in the black with the square-cut neck and white organdie collar. Hadn't there been talk somewhere, though, just about that? 'Way back somewhere. Women can get away with murder. Screens around ankles. Of course! She and Martin. It wouldn't be nice, — it wouldn't be right, to wear the black with the square-cut neck. But why? It was so hard to think. Poor Deneen, showing her the newspaper cuts of herself and trying to make her understand the wisdom of wearing the black dress that somehow made her seem so small and so very, very white. So pitiably small.

"Good God, girl, help me. Cash in on your natural good points. You have to counteract, with all the personality appeal in the world, these articles that have so stirred up public opinion. You're innocent and you must look it. You're beautiful, and you must show it. You've legitimate weapons, and you must

use them. Let the district attorney yodel and
scream and dervish his way through this
trial. We've the cold dramatic material of
truth in our hands."

Yes. Yes. Of course. Poor Mr. Deneen.
The hours of the drilling and the rehearsing
for the drama. The drama of the big scene.
The big scene of taking the witness chair.
O God, let me care enough. Don't let my
brain fall to little pieces. Let me care what
happens to me. Martin out there, dearest
dear. The eyes of the Lighthouse. The dear
eyes of the Lighthouse. O God, help me
out of this numbness. So much is at stake.
The doctors yesterday, showing how the
dagger must have been plunged. Why did
you let me turn him over that night, God?
The terrible, terrible twisting of the truth
about the party that night by Mrs. Snuggs.
The frown on the face of the Walrus as he
listened to Mrs. Snuggs. The Walrus believing
Mrs. Snuggs!

There had never been such a frown on the
face of the Walrus as when he listened to
Mrs. Snuggs; for that matter, on the whole
row of them. They had been frowning so
after Mrs. Snuggs, and after the doctors had
said that it must have been plunged. You
in Mr. Terry's lap at the party. Oh, Mrs.

Snuggs, how could you? Help me to tell them it was not like that. The two rows of jury there without any legs. The rose-quartz dagger had been plunged in, said the wise doctors. The doctor who looked like Shakespeare. The potato of a doctor on toothpick legs. Help me to make them see. I tell you, all-twelve-of-you-from-the-waist-up, I rolled him over! I turned him face up. You, out there. Bloated sea. You in the jury-box. You hear! If only I had not rolled him over, you would have understood. But I didn't know, you see. He lay there so still. Martin, dear Martin, can't you help me? I'm so tired — Martin ——

*

Couldn't drag in the legs that were made of granite. The numb legs of the graven image. The legs that were to lead to the witness chair. Couldn't. Couldn't.

"You have nothing to fear. With your simple and straightforward directness, you are going to tear down the structure of false evidence that has been built up against you."

You have nothing to fear. That was right. How could one to whom nothing meant anything have fear? And yet Martin, dear, dear Martin, with his face pulled that way on the stretcher, and dear, dear eyes of the Lighthouse, there was pain to fear for them.

Never in the history of the trial had there been such a sea of faces. The boiling sea of them being pushed back by the officers with clubs. Figures clinging to the high window-sills like flies. Smell of humanity. Rushings. Comings. Goings. The running-down aisles of the clerks and the stenographers and the court attendants. The buckling and the un-buckling of brief-cases. Scrapings of chairs. The sea boiling this morning to a high tide. The high tide of expectancy. The high tide of climax. The high tide of the defendant about to take the chair.

The State *versus* Orchid Sargossa. Fancy that. The great big State and just Orchid Sargossa. Of Nana, in Prince Street. Nana too must have been a dream.

Where is Martin? Stop. Stop. They must stop pinioning him against the wall. Poor Martin in the crush. And the Eyes. There they were in the third row left. Dear eyes. Strange and frantic eyes. I didn't do it, Eyes. Martin knows I didn't, but Martin doesn't care whether I did it or not. That's my Martin. Martin doesn't care. Isn't that won-derful! Eyes, why is it you care so terribly, when I don't care?

Deneen whispering. Deneen whispering. "Keep your pluck and your nerve and your head, and remember you have nothing to fear. You have the situation in your hands. Tear down their false testimony. Remember every point you must score. Emphasize. Don't forget, dear Miss Sargossa, please don't forget, to explain in your own way, precisely as you explained it to me, just how Mrs. Snuggs happened to find you seated on Terry's lap that night of the party. You were dragged there. You were struggling to get free. Fight back against the lying old landlady's testimony. Make them see the way you rolled the body over. Lay your heart bare. You are your best defence, Miss Sargossa. Fight. Fight your way into the twelve hearts of the twelve jurors."

Fight. If only there was a way, instead, just to crumple down into sleep and then wake up somewhere — far — in a garden ——

The district attorney was shouting again. It was horrible. He was all screwed up like a howling dervish. A howling dervish. What was that? Deneen called him that. Reference-room. Why, one daren't go to the reference-room any more. Think of that! Clanking of keys.

Now, who had gone and plumped you down

so hard in the yellow chair with the arms?
The same chair that Mrs. Snuggs had sat herself down in. The witness chair, of course.
The wet lips of the women out there in the
sea. The faces of men propped up on collar-
points. The boiling sea that had turned into a
frozen sea. Martin, don't let them jam you so
back there against that wall. The Eyes —
don't let them go out on me now. Mr. Deneen.
Let me be. I know what I want to say.

"Your Honour, this is the whole, the simple
truth of the way the thing happened."

"You will have to speak louder, Miss
Sargossa. Swing a little around toward the
Jury."

"YOUR HONOR, THIS IS THE WAY
THE THING HAPPENED ——"

There was somebody sitting down in the
bottom of a dry cistern, talking in a cold,
clear, hollow-sounding way. It was you, sitting in the middle of the cistern, and the
cistern was the frozen sea.

"You see, your Honour, my entire life has
been what you might say, well, I mean,
my mother, as you know, my mother,
while she was kind to me, somehow she was
not — well, what shall I say?"

"Go on, Miss Sargossa, you are doing very
well."

Drone. Drone. Drone. What would Mr.
Deneen say? She was forgetting all the coaching, the moments to be dramatic, the part
about the violets for Cyd and the evenings
in the reference-room. One was to get worked
up enough to cry for the jury. And here she
was, only talking to the Judge instead. So
very simply. The big kind eyes of the Judge,
they looked down upon her exactly like two
faithful watch-dogs to be held in leash. The
leash of any possible emotion. Oh, dear Mr.
Deneen, don't be angry. I want to be dramatic, but it's all too terrible to be dramatic about. And I am sitting in a cistern
talking to the Judge, and no other words
will come. The simple words of the simple
truth. Isn't that what you said? Don't you
think they will understand? The Walrus,
the Tomato, and the Slatt, the twelve of the
jurors? Sing a song of sixpence, four-and-
twenty blackbirds baked in a pie. No, no,
no. "As I was saying, your Honour ——"

Well, there you were out of the yellow oak
chair, and Mr. Deneen was whispering and
patting your hand, and the sea of bloated
faces was full of the flutter of handkerchiefs.

"I forgot so much. Please, Mr. Deneen,
I couldn't think. I couldn't see. Only, maybe
the Judge — he knew ——"

"It's all right ——"

"I forgot the part where ——"

"It's all right. You did better than the dramatic thing: you did the simple, true thing."

Why, the Eyes! The Eyes of the Lighthouse were shining with wetness. And where was Martin? Martin was gone from where they had him pinioned to the wall, and the sea was moving again, and boiling.

And now, Bang. Bang. Bang. The district attorney was summing up. Martin, where are you? I need you now. He's summing up. Bang. Bang. The twisted face. The screwing face. The twisted, screwing face, untwisting and making everything sound horrible. Why, those words were Martin's words! Your words and Martin's words! Hey, you, those are Martin's words!

Give the woman murderer her chance to take her punishment like a man — that is your true sex equality. Don't let the women of this country literally get away with murder — let the woman of to-day fall or stand on her own. She will have more respect for you — the women of America must secretly despise the male jury; they must laugh up their sleeves at the spectacle of a judge ordering a screen placed around the ankles of the fair defendant. You men, you citizens, you fathers of families, can you sit back and see not only yourselves made ridiculous, but your government travestied and the well-being of this democracy imperilled on the rock of sex-sentimentality? Two doctors have told you, gesture by gesture, how this woman plunged a rapier into a moving, beating heart — the heart of a man. Is sex equality a joke?

Why, Martin, those are your very words. The words we talked out together back there in the dear old unbelievably remote days. Martin, is that what you call the pyre you have built under us? But isn't it fine that the district attorney and everybody should be quoting you! Martin, I'm proud of you. Bang. Bang. Bang. The district attorney was still summing up. One must listen. The terrible district attorney shouting at the jury. The frowning jury.

"Men, you, this is a case of justice, not sex. See that you do not fail in your sense of duty, of honour, and of fair play by condoning this murder just because it was committed by a woman. If this woman goes free, you are as guilty as she is."

And now, Mr. Deneen, your turn! Dear kind Mr. Deneen, pleading for me. Thank

you — oh, thank you for telling them that.
I forgot! I wanted them to know the horribleness of Mr. Terry holding me down on his
knee. Not like Mrs. Snuggs said, though.
That's right, tell them! I was beating him
off, not patting him. Dear Mr. Deneen, make
them understand that. Tell them, too, how
I rolled him over. Tell them that again and
again. Tell them about my Nana. Poor old
Nana. Maybe that will help. Dear, good,
kind Mr. Deneen, all of the things I couldn't
tell them about down in the cistern, you tell
them for me now. About the horribleness of
him, and how he fell on it. Oh, Mr. Deneen,
make them believe. God, you help him to
make them believe.

No wonder there was such a hush. That
was His Honour speaking. The tired, harassed-looking Judge was using some of
Martin's words, too. That made Orchid feel
proud. The Judge did not thunder. He was —
how was it they put it? — ah yes, the Judge
was admonishing the jury.

Gentlemen of the jury . . . charge you
. . . solemn duty . . . the State . . . God
. . . bring to bear upon your judgments . . .
every ounce . . . unbiased . . . sex equality
a farce or a reality (that was Martin's) . . .
true to man- and woman-kind (Martin's!).

MANNEQUIN

. . . Look deeply into your own hearts . . . ask yourselves . . . incriminate . . . malice aforethought . . . premeditated crime . . . hysteria of passion . . . accidental . . . weigh, men, weigh. . . .

The Judge was like a mountain. He was superb. And the sea was listening to the mountain, and the mountain was looking at the sea. The Lighthouse, too, was gleaming at the mountain.

Oh, how the Lighthouse was gleaming at the mountain. . . .

Jury, I admonish you, in the name of justice, fair play, man's humanity to man — and woman. . . . You are about to retire into a session involving the gravest responsibility man can impose upon man . . . human life . . . in your hands . . . be wise . . . be honest . . . God-fearing . . . human life in the balance. . . . Do unto others . . . careful . . . unbiased . . . solemn duty . . . God's will. . . .

Dear Judge, where are they going — the Walrus, the Tomato, and the Slatt? Out there to decide about me? Life. Death. Dear Judge. Am I fainting, or is it that the Lighthouse in the third row is toppling over? There go the Walrus, the Tomato, and the Slatt. See, see, Lighthouse, Martin, Judge, let's all of us try not to laugh — there go the Walrus, the Tomato, and the Slatt.

*

Four-and-twenty blackbirds baked in a pie. When the pie was opened the birds began to sing. Wasn't that a dainty — dish — to — set — before —— No, no, no. One simply must keep one's mind on the dreadful track of reality! Orchid in the corner of her cell of cot-basin-and-bucket. She had receded into it like a bit of fungus clinging to granitoid wall. Forty-nine hours of sitting waiting for the four-and-twenty blackbirds — no, no, no — forty-nine hours of waiting for the twelve men of the jury to decide.

To decide what? If only one's mind wouldn't fuddle up so. Of course: to decide if you had murdered Mr. Terry. You, who always stepped out of the way of little ants scurrying for sidewalk cracks, accused of murdering Mr. Terry!

Why all this deciding, when just in a few words you could tell them how it all came about? Oh, why hadn't you, in those few precious moments when you had the witness chair, why hadn't you told them then, clearly enough to make them understand?

During those forty-nine hours of the terror

of waiting she could have torn open her heart
for the words. The words that must somehow,
in some way, explain to the twelve of them
locked in there the way that the cape was
torn from her shoulders. The cape that tinkled
with the clanking of keys. No, no, not the
clanking of keys. The cape that tinkled with
the tiny sword dangling from its jewelled
scabbard. Mr. Terry had fallen forward on
it and pierced himself to the heart. There
must be a way to make the twelve men know
that. And she had rolled him over!

Why would they not believe that? Life
meant so little; and yet, how terrible that
there was no way to show them the truth!
To show the Lighthouse the truth.

*

The jury was open at the collar, and Mr.
Baker, who was the butcher, kept sucking
ice with great draughty noises.

It was so very hot, and after forty-nine
hours of disagreement Baker and Duvonnie
had developed the habit of plunging forward
into the crooks of their arms for impromptu
naps on the table, and that kept Mr. Fudge
in a more or less constant state of gavel-gavel,
Gentlemen!

Forty-nine hours of locked-up conference

in a room into which Sewell and Mix and Longini and Slatt and a fellow named Laucheim had lighted forty-nine hours of end-on-end cigars, cigarettes, and stogies.

It was the bloodshot stage, the swollen-eyed stage. Even Mr. Fudge, who was thin to cadaverousness, had sacs of bloated flesh under his eyes.

"Gentlemen of the jury, unless Mr. Baker can be induced to join with us in consensus of opinion, I see little hope of getting out of here to-day."

"Gentlemen, I am joost so anxious as you are. I got my wive. I got my business, joost like you. But only because I am an honest man have I got them. Only because I am an honest man am I on this jury. And because I am an honest man I must hold out for what I belief."

"Yes, Mr. Baker, we respect your convictions. But so are all of the gentlemen of this jury honest men. But, like courageous men, they have dared to change their minds."

"Dot voman, so sure like I sit here, dot cold liddle voman, mit blue pieces of ice for eyes, murdered dot man. The landlady! Dot's ven I know it for sure. Paddy-cakes on laps — goings-on like dot — lead to joost what happened."

[282]

"But, Mr. Baker ——"

"Gentlemen, if I haf eleven against me and I want joost like you to go home to my wive, my front borch, and my business, no voman mit a pair of blue eyes and such a sweet liddle shyness mit the jury gets me on dot. A murder is a murder, gentlemen. It don't matter a man or a voman. In such a gountry like ours, a voman, she gets away with murder. All you got to do is joost to put a screen around her ankles ——"

"All right. All right. Let's not go over that again. Sure as my name is Duvonnie that woman didn't murder that rotter. He fell on the dagger."

"Course he did. Why, Baker, I should think your knowledge of human nature would tell you that much. When that little person got up there on the stand and told her story as simply as a child, without one desire for effect or dramatics, what further evidence of her innocence can you need than the evidence of your own eyes as she stood before us? A simple, honest, frightened child. An innocent child."

"If we are to start that all over again, gentlemen ——"

"Say, looka here, Baker, you're no better than the rest of us. I come into this room

forty-nine hours ago, and wouldn't 'a' given
you a Canadian dime for that woman's chances.
I had my doubts. Big doubts. I wasn't going
to let her simplicity stuff get me, neither.
I was ready for conviction. So were seven
of these other gentlemen. But threshing it
out this way, we've seen the light. That
little woman's evidence stacks up too high
in her favour. That little woman didn't
murder that guy."

"Dot's joost it! Dot *liddle* voman. Would
it be dot *liddle* man? If dot *liddle* voman was
a man instead of a ——"

"Aw, forget it. You talk like an Innesbrook newspaper, Baker."

Gavel-gavel. "Not so fast, gentlemen,"
said Mr. Fudge, and reached out a long lean
forefinger.

"If you ask me, I think that young fellow
in the witness chair day before yesterday
about hit it right, only they shut him up.
That guy had the right idea. He says this
case can turn into a pernicious example of
baiting the woman. Public hysteria has swung
too far. This here jury is afraid *not* to convict
Orchid Sargossa. Well, by Gad, I'm not
afraid. And I'll tell the world so. I'm not
afraid, and I defy any man's man of you here
to admit he's afraid!"

"No. No. No, siree!"

"Remember, Mr. Baker, the conditions under which this jury has worked have been most unusual. Maybe you don't realize it, but just about the very day this whole thing broke, the newspapers were beginning to stir up agitation about the women of the country being able to get away with murder. The Scott case and all those just fresh in people's mind. Don't let the pendulum swing too far, Mr. Baker. As that fellow said, a jury may be afraid *not* to convict Orchid Sargossa, whether she is guilty or innocent."

"Vell, I don't say maybe such an opinion ain't right, too. I vouldn't vant, gentlemen, I should be the one to be afraid ——"

"Exactly, Mr. Baker. And just as surely as I am foreman of this jury we will be branded as cowards if we convict this girl. We are taking a human life into our hands on a wave of prejudice, wasn't that the way that young fellow who wrote some of those articles put it when he was in the witness chair yesterday? on a wave of public hysteria that has swung too far."

"Vell, I don't say ——"

"Of course you don't, Mr. Baker," shouted Mr. Duvonnie, who had a trigger-like quickness which he had used to advantage in breaking down previous oppositions of this jury. "Of course you don't! If, after the evidence we have stacked on this table before us, you still hold out against the eleven men of this jury for the guilt of the girl, then you are deliberately allowing yourself to be swayed by mob hysteria. That's a great phrase, that is. Says it all in a nutshell. You are condemning a human soul to destruction because you are hysterical with mob psychology. That's it, you are hysterical with mob psychology. Shame."

"I——"

"Gentlemen of the jury, are you content to see this member of our jury brand us as a group of hystericals? A jury that is afraid *not* to convict this woman? Are we going to let him continue to lock this jury, when eleven out of the twelve men in this room agree that Orchid Sargossa is innocent of murder as interpreted by the court?"

*

It was outrageous, and Selene knew it, but cried because the Judge was stern and curt with her.

The heat came in waves into the Judge's antechamber. The Judge, with his gown dangling on a hanger on the back of the door,

[286]

paced up and down in an alpaca coat, mopping his face. Someone, this stenographer or that court attendant, was constantly making a gurgling sound by turning on the spigot of the water-cooler that stood between the windows. Two electric fans hummed.

"John Lester, couldn't you send in and ask how soon ——"

"For God's sake, Selene, if you ask me that again I'll go mad. I have told you everything I know. The last word was that an agreement was about to be reached. I don't propose to send and inquire again. Since you insist upon remaining here, you will know as soon as I when the word comes to call court and receive the foreman's spoken verdict. This is beyond all reason. You need a doctor."

"Do you think, dear, the jury will ——"

"I don't think. I'm too harassed to think. Why in heaven's name, on a day like this when she could rest at home in peace and cool and quiet, any woman in her senses would insist upon dragging herself into town is beyond me."

"Maybe, it may be, dear, that — I — I'm not in my senses."

"Maybe you're not, Selene. It's a cruel thing to say, but the way you have been acting these past weeks, it's difficult to understand how you could be!"

"But, John, dear ———"

"As if I haven't been harassed enough! and now, just before I must hold court to receive an important verdict, you throw me into a fresh state of nervousness."

"Even you, then, John, admit that it is important. And if you say that, what must it be to me?"

"What do you mean by that? What must it be to you, except that a woman is to be freed if innocent, or convicted if guilty? What else can it mean to you?"

"I — I don't know, John — except ———"

"Yes, exactly; you don't know, except. Really, my dear Selene, what has come over you?"

"I don't know, John. I don't know, John — only — let me stay, John — close to you— I'm silly, dear, but — but humour me ———"

It was impossible for him to hold out against her. He must get her away, now that the case was over. To the seaside. Europe. Was it possible that Selene was really going back into the state of nervous decline? Harassed Judge Herrick, waiting for word to call court and receive the verdict of the jury.

MANNEQUIN

*

The only perception really left to Annie Pogany was the visual. Curious and rather merciful, how the eyesight had persisted. Smell and even taste had gone long ago. And sometimes, because her fingers were like clubs, and her arms all punctured with tiny holes, it was quite a little while before Annie, once an object was in her hands, could feel its shape or texture or temperature.

It did not matter much, because hers was largely a matter of the struggle for existence to obtain the one object that she recognized immediately by sight. The sight that her eyes were greedy for, and that they could still shine and connive for.

There was that object, a bottle, in her hands now, as she sat on a bench in a patch of park along a waterfront. She had slept on that bench. That is, she had slept on several such benches, between shovings-along by policemen.

There was not much left of Annie. She was as terrible and as picked and as gaunt as an old crow. Women like Annie peck about like old crows, too. At wastage. The wastage in ash-cans, in garbage-pails, and in débris.

And Annie herself was débris. A bit of

it there on the edge of life. Annie sitting there with her gin-bottle a bit groggily, and reading a scrap of newspaper. A stained ugly bit of anybody's newspaper, left lying on the bench.

Stalking old crow of an Annie, about to stalk out of life. You felt it instinctively, old-crow Annie sitting there on the edge of park and the edge of life, reading the stained old newspaper.

It was not so much the face: it was the set of the head on the shoulders. For at least an hour, shuddering constantly of an ague to which she was subject, and fumbling the discoloured thing she wore as scarf closer to her shoulders, as of cold, Annie sat regarding the newspaper picture of the set of that head on those shoulders.

Annie knew those shoulders! They were the shoulders of the Orchid who had been hers.

There was no name. A stain had dyed it out. Cunning Annie, though. Everything was torn away except a bit of the printed matter: "Verdict expected to-day. Municipal Court Building . . . crowds . . . unusual interest aroused by. . . ."

Cunning Annie. Most of the cunning in her instilled into fires by the swigs from the gin-bottle. Fires that would presently die down, leaving her as black as a cave after a bonfire.

Cunning old stalking crow. Those shoulders were dear to her. Municipal Court Building. It was difficult to get the policemen to reply to her when she stood asking. It was easier to wait for kindly-faced women who paused, directed her, and sometimes dropped pennies into the crook of her palm.

Municipal Court Building. . . .

*

Why, there were the faces again! Orchid knew many of them now, by sight and name. Oh, oh, stop pushing. Why, this is outrageous! The shoving and battling of all the policemen with their clubs. Watch out, there! That woman has a baby in her arms. Stop it!

Yes, the faces again. The face of the red-haired stenographer who all through the trial had written left-handed, and all the reporters with their scribbling fingers, and the attendant who bawled out the names. Mrs. Emanie Snuggs. Miss Toto Stroheim. There was Toto herself, with her face like a mask with slits in it for eyes. And Cyd in a mannish silk blouse. Why, there were everybody. Max

Innesbrook, himself, fanning with a Panama hat. Where was Martin? There was the Lighthouse all right, but where was Martin?

She was once more the bit of fungus clinging to the corner of her chair. Presently, as always during the days of the eternity, the Judge who was a mountain came in and bowed to the sea, and the sea rose.

The mountain was looking at the sea.

More passings in and out of the stenographers and the messengers, and the Judge reading slips of paper, and the tiptoeing around of the stenographers, and the whisperings between Deneen and the reporters, and the district attorney with his face all set now, as if his mouth were a bolt drawn across his face.

Why don't they come? Please, why? The four-and-twenty blackbirds — no, no, the twelve jurymen. Why don't they come, please? The Lighthouse must have been asking that, too. Her eyes never swerved from the door.

There they came! The four-and-twenty, no, no, twelve. The Walrus, the Tomato, and the Slatt. Don't let me faint. There they were. Mountain looking at sea. Where was Martin? There was Max Innesbrook all right, fanning himself with the Panama.

Why, no, Max was riding a bicycle, and his head was wrapped in a Turkish towel — riding a bicycle to nowhere. Lighthouse, help me ——

"Your Honour, this jury has the honour to report that it finds the prisoner at the bar not guilty."

You were tumbling down a hillside — a hill made of the clapping of hands.

*

Almost before she came to, she was ashamed and sheepish at having lost consciousness.

"I'm so sorry. Where do I go now?" I'll go. Clank. Clank. Back to the corridors of the grating of the keys. No?

The Lighthouse was fanning something. Fanning Orchid. And Martin, with his collar open, was holding a tumbler of water, and the Judge had off his robe and was standing in the farthest part of the room talking to Max Innesbrook, but looking at Orchid. And now, why, there were Martin and Max Innesbrook shaking hands, and Martin flushing up and lopping the water over the sides of the tumbler. The way he would do it, dear silly. And, shaking hands again, Martin and his uncle.

Dear Lighthouse. But of course she had

only actually said: "I'm so sorry. Where do I go now?"

"You're in the Judge's chambers, dear child."

"I guess I must have fainted — the heat ——."

"I guess you must have."

"And this? What is this in a box? A fountain-pen. Oh yes, the Walrus. And the medicine-dropper, too. Well, well. Yes, I — guess I must have fainted."

"John Lester, Martin, here, let us help her up."

Everybody milling around. Shaking hands, and Martin squeezing your hands so that the damp fingers clung together and you had to pull them apart. Martin, your collar, dear. The district attorney with the bolt of his mouth drawn back, smiling and shaking hands with Deneen. And then, actually, with you. Bad Martin, to have made your fingers stick in clumps, when you had to shake hands with the district attorney. And Mr. Deneen kissing you on the hair. Everybody congratulating everybody. And Martin, who should have been solemn, standing there with his collar open like a gate on a broken hinge, blushing and having his hand pumped by his uncle. Dear Martin, there had been the heaviest tears in his eyes when you first woke out of the faint; and now there he was blustering.

"You mustn't slip away from me now, after everything is over, Miss Sargossa."

That was the Lighthouse talking. The Lighthouse was saying that!

"Dear Mrs. Lighthouse, no, no, dear Mrs. Herrick, if not for you, through all the days — you and Martin ——"

"I know, Orchid."

"I knew that you knew."

"The Judge, Orchid, even though he would never let me mention it to him, I knew that he knew, too."

"And I knew that he knew. Dear you, who are you?"

"What?"

"Nothing. I — I guess I'm a little befuddled. I must be, or I wouldn't be seeing her. Out there. Please, Mrs. Herrick, look! Do you see her too, or am I befuddled? No. No. Don't chase her out. Let her come in. That's my Nana! You let her in, you! Nana! That's my Nana, the one I was telling you about!"

The old crow, the terrible old crow, there in Orchid's arms, full of croaking noises, and Orchid crying into them.

"Why, Nana, my poor Nana. They brought me your hat. It seemed the hat of someone drowned. This is my Nana, Mrs. Herrick — my poor old drift of a Nana."

The eyes of Selene. The revolted strangely grudging eyes of Selene.

"Nana, where have you been, to get yourself like this?" The straggle of hair in grey clumps. The ruin of a hat. The weather-stained skirt that had literally dragged in bilge-water. The discoloured rag of a scarf.

Orchid, who loathed a stained thing, with her cheek up against that scarf. And suddenly Selene, with a hand that was predatory, leaping out to snatch the scarf off the shoulders of Annie Pogany.

"You!" she called out, as if she were talking to someone on the opposite side of a swift river. "You! Where did you get that scarf? John Lester, that scarf! Red berries — Ho-Ho birds — there — see, behind the dirt. Where did you get that scarf? You! You! *Annie Pogany!*"

All the rivers of the world were standing still. The rivers of the blood. That was how Orchid felt on that cry of "Annie Pogany." Not because of the cry, but because of the face of Selene, eyeing that dirty rag of scarf.

Poor old crow. She began to croak then

to Selene, the two of them standing in the centre of the circle of bystanders.

The croaking and the croaking of Annie, and the stock-still look of the Judge, who was standing beside Selene, and the stock-still stunned look of Martin. Dear Martin, give me your hand — I — why, Martin, why, Martin, button your collar, Martin — I — why, Martin, the crow and the Lighthouse are talking of me, or is it just the way my ear-drums beat?

Selene was so quiet when she turned. Only the Judge and Martin, beside Orchid, really heard:

"You remember the day I showed you through the house, Joan? Your room was the one I didn't unlock. The south room, with the sunshine waiting in it."

A NOTE ON THE TYPE IN
WHICH THIS BOOK IS SET

The type in which this book has been set (on the Monotype) is Garamond. This face is an adaptation by Frederick W. Goudy, of a type designed by Claude Garamont in the sixteenth century. A pupil of Geofroy Tory, Garamont was the foremost type designer and letter cutter of his time (1510–1561). It is believed that he based his letters on the Venetian models although he has introduced a number of important differences, and it is to Garamont that we owe the letter which we know as Old Style. In adapting this type to modern usage Mr. Goudy has not attempted an exact duplication of any of the Garamont models, and he has combined all the characteristics of the original design with the unmistakable Goudy touch.

SET UP AND ELECTROTYPED BY THE PLIMPTON
PRESS, NORWOOD, MASS. PRINTED BY THE
VAN REES PRESS, NEW YORK. ESPARTO
PAPER MANUFACTURED IN SCOTLAND
AND FURNISHED BY W. F. ETHER-
INGTON & CO., NEW YORK.
BOUND BY THE H. WOLFF ES-
TATE, NEW YORK. TITLE
PAGE DESIGNED BY
ELMER ADLER